SEEDS OF CONVICTION

CORE: BOOK TWO

BY

MAQUEL A. JACOB

Published by
MAJart Works
Hillsboro, Oregon
https://www.majartworks.com

Cover Art by Dar Albert
www.wickedsmartdesigns.com

ACKNOWLEDGMENTS

Thank you so much for your continued interest in the Core Trilogy. I hope you enjoy the second installment and get ready for more in book three, Bonds of Contrition, which will bring our story to its end.

A huge thank you to NaNoWriMo, (National Novel Writing Month), for having a platform to support writers' creative juices and help keep me on track. Without them I would not have met Dr. Laurel Standley, who contributes in more ways than I can express and introduced me to NIWA.

Big ginormous hugs to all my writer peeps at NIWA (Northwest Independent Writer's Association). You keep me honest and I have more fun each time we get together. To all who supported me and read Book One, the wait is over. It took longer than anticipated, but better late than never.

To my early stage beta readers: my sincere condolences and immense gratitude.

ONE:

Spy on Earth

High above the charred remains of cities worldwide, the last alien warships ascended into Earth's atmosphere. Humans battling with planet Azrom's rebel faction had come to a screeching halt. It was fierce and bloody with casualties disproportionate on the human's side but somehow, every mutant Azrom enforcer had been wiped out. A mixture of relief and sorrow swept through the inhabitants of Earth with only a select few from each respective party knowing why.

The Razznian spy, dressed in a hooded track suit that hid his scaly skinned body, watched with curiosity as the humans struggled to comprehend the mass destruction left behind from a battle they didn't start. His lidless red eyes scanned the area and his mouth opened to reveal two rows of razor sharp teeth. An equivalent of a smile. Observing, but not interacting with the battle proved to be a good idea.

He had watched Azrom's armada supporting another alien group on the ground and upon closer look, realized they were Lassian. The race supposedly extinct by Azrom supreme ruler's, Halfar, own hands.

How could they be here, and in such large numbers?

He made his way to the rendezvous point where a portal back to Razzna sat open for his departure. There was a lot to report on.

Home Coming

The sky churned viciously as the Azromian Armada's mother ship made an angled descent through the stratosphere. All six thrusters rotated, maneuvering beneath its underbelly in preparation for landing. Air concaved around the gunmetal hull covered with large spikes as it emerged from the clouds. Correcting its position perpendicular to the ground below, created winds with enough force to bend nearby trees and rattle the palace foundations.

Halfar watched, from the command center of the ship, palace guards rush forward onto the roof to await his arrival. In full battle gear, he stood arms folded with legs wide apart while the surriunding crew focused on controlling the ship. Being back on his home world sent a shiver through him. There was a lot of work to accomplish to rectify the damage done by his advisors, now deceased. He had dispatched them as a ruler was obligated to do.

The invasion and conquering of Earth, instigated by his advisors with General Kur as a scapegoat, turned into rescuing the human race from his own Armada. Assistance came from warriors of planet Lassa via their leader, Chardon. After the battle ended, the gate to Earth had been severed. Humankind was not ready for interaction with technologically advanced alien races.

More damage had been done to his soul and that of his soldiers than anything else. The loss and regret spread wide among his people and the Lassians, who he had nearly made extinct. It was a mess he alone had to correct over the next few decades. Right now, he needed a plan for rebuilding his council and the trust of his generals.

With a roar and crushing winds, the ship settled into a hover over the palace platform. A small square of light opened at the underbelly and shot down a few hundred feet from the waiting entourage. The light rescinded and in its place stood Halfar with his two Generals, Rass and Kur, flanking him on each side followed by a handful of enforcers. Everyone's hair whipped into their faces as the ship moved laterally across the sky towards the docking bay ten miles to the east.

The guards dropped down in unison to one knee, bowing their heads while laying their left arm across the thigh, the other hand flat on the ground in front of them. Halfar grimaced at the display. He hadn't witnessed the perfect triangular formation of his guards in full regalia for some time. Glancing at Kur he saw the twinkle of delight in his eyes. Rass seemed unimpressed, for he didn't acknowledge the greeting. After a few moments, the guards stood back up and the leader came forward to address Halfar directly.

"My lord, it is good to see you again. It has been too long." He bowed his head again.

"Yes, a shame it has to be on these circumstances."

"Indeed." The leader's face scrunched up as if he had smelled something rotten. Halfar motioned towards the door leading into the palace and the guards about faced, parting like the red sea to allow passage. "How long will you be staying this time, my lord?" He tried to keep up with Halfar's fast pace while conversing.

"At the least, until I elect a new council and assure the progress of rebuilding."

As the entourage passed the guards at the palace entry, Halfar saw slight movement out of the corner of his eye and witnessed Rass attempt to stop himself from stumbling by reaching out to place his hand on a wall nearby. His injuries were minor but the mental anguish he suffered had manifested as physical pain. Kur caught him by the elbow on impulse. It occurred in mere seconds and no one else noticed. He worried about both his young Generals.

The doors to the throne room were opened by two guards to reveal a massive hall built like a large cave made of golden Amber rock. Torches along the walls gave it a coppery glow. Giant columns the color of sandstone spaced twenty feet apart from each other stood majestic connecting to the ceiling.

Entering the throne room, Halfar motioned for servants with his hand and twenty of them appeared lining up in two rows on either side of the hall. He proceeded to his rightful seat, taking the stone steps two at a time, and turned to face the entrance before plopping down in a heap. Rass and Kur came up to take their place on either side of him. A servant advanced towards the throne and Halfar waved him forward, whispering instructions in his ear. The servant stepped back, bowed low, and left the hall taking four other servants with him.

"My Lord, is there anything you require of your royal guards at this moment?" The captain of the guard stood at attention in the entryway.

"No, keep watch of the gateway portal and wait for another arrival."

"My Lord?" The Captain raised one eyebrow.

"I have," Halfar hesitated for a moment. This was a delicate matter. "Acquired a mate."

There was a palpable silence as the news took hold. Halfar had never taken a mate before or had any interest in procreating for that matter. A mate now seemed a bit too sudden for them.

"She should be arriving two moons from now with a small group and," Halfar sighed heavily knowing this would be yet another shock, "my son." He heard the gasps.

"Congratulations, My Lord!" They all shouted in unison. "A royal heir is to be celebrated." The Captain announced.

"Yes, yes. When they arrive, we will discuss the details." Halfar waved them away.

When the guards exited the throne room, the doors thundering shut, Kur turned to him and tsked. He was rewarded with a look of disgust complete with narrowed eyes.

"My Lord, divulging such matters on the first day is irresponsible of you. You could have at least waited a moon cycle to spring it."

"It would not have mattered either way."

The male servant from earlier returned with the other four carrying various trays of food and refreshments. Each tray was laid at the edge of the throne's platform. He carried two large cushions on top of his head for the two generals. It was not a moment too soon. Rass eased himself down onto the cushion set beside him and went into a near fetal position. Kur sat down cross legged on his and glanced over with a worried expression.

"Leave us," Halfar ordered. The other servants along the walls hesitated. He knew why. Their ruler should never be left unattended but at the moment he had no patience for it. "Now!" He watched them all flee through the inner chamber doors on the far side of the hall.

Making sure the last one was far gone, Halfar pushed himself off his throne and crawled over to Rass. He checked his breathing by laying a hand on his chest to feel the rise and fall of it. Rass did not stir from the touch. Halfar saw Kur's shadow fall over them.

Stealthy as ever.

He brushed some of Rass' hair away from his face and stood up next to Kur. They both looked at each other; Halfar contemplating, Kur accusatory.

In the previous battle before their return, Halfar had given Rass the mission of eliminating Kur, who had acted in what he thought was treason. Knowing their past history as lovers, it must have seemed especially cruel given Kur's situation. The act in itself caused Rass to mentally break and Halfar knew he was to blame. The following months afterwards on New Lassa found Kur trying to repair their damaged relationship.

"He is in no shape to deal with the reforming of the regiments." Kur stated the obvious.

"Then you have to deal with it along with inspection of the battle ships."

"That leaves you to do what, exactly?"

"Deal with the remaining council members who weren't stupid enough to go against me."

"Ahh, well I bid you success."

"First, we rest a bit." Halfar went back to his throne. "You will stay with him for a while after I leave?" Kur's face scrunched up as he turned to him. "Should I not have bothered to ask?" He eased back and began to ponder how to rectify the damage done.

Assessments

Chardon surveyed the landscape of New Lassa for the best options to make it more habitable. Their original home world had been destroyed, scorched black, by a planet bomb sent by Halfar. An event regretted by all involved. Scientists from both races were now in the works collaborating to find a remedy for the planet's weak sun. A brighter sun meant more heat and better vegetation. So far, the highest temperature during the warm season reached a mere 21 degrees Celsius. The eyes of everyone on the planet over the past few decades started changing to accommodate its light.

Loud screeching from across the fields made Chardon's head snap up and turn towards the sound. It meant one thing; her son was being teased by one of the older manbeasts. She smiled at that. If not by Mota, then possibly Trinon. Both were the sons of her personal guardian, Modas. Soon, she would travel to Azrom to stay with her mate, Halfar, for a little while with one of them in tow.

The visit was more like a war council than a family reunion. Chardon's previous mate, Sestis, had set into motion a string of events that threatened both Lassa and Azrom. For battle with their new joint enemy, Razzna, they needed to combine forces and hope for victory. The planning should only take a decade at most. Razznians were a nasty species who fought with no sense of honor for the simple fact they were not as strong as they appeared.

Off in the distance, a tall male figure advanced towards her. As he got closer, she immediately knew who it was. His brown sandy colored mane hung down to the back of his knees, swaying in the breeze. What started as a tiny smile grew, spreading across his angelic face as he caught sight of Chardon, steely blue eyes reflecting the sunlight. He was wearing a full tunic suit with the undone robe flapping around his six foot five-inch muscled frame.

"Trinon," Chardon started to ask his question.

"Hmm?" Even at a distance, a manbeasts' hearing was impeccable.

"Was that you torturing my son earlier?"

Trinon's smile turned into a big wide grin.

"No, not at all."

He stopped a few feet from Chardon and his eyes averted away. All he had to do next was stick his tongue out and Chardon would have smacked him. It was something Trinon became fond of doing lately to appear innocent and cheeky.

"Really?" Chardon's brow lifted.

"Well," Trinon turned back to look down at her, "Mota began the prodding, and, well."

"Explain yourselves."

"We wanted to see if he could climb the monolith."

Trinon's tongue slipped out between his lips and Chardon reached up to grab it with the intention of harm, but Trinon was faster bobbing sideways to the right.

"He's not a man beast," Chardon chided him.

"Close enough," a new voice replied from behind Trinon.

Mota came up to them with Chardon's son, Farin, in tow. He was only an inch or two taller than Trinon even though he was much older. They were resembling their father more as the years went on. Mota set Farin down and brushed some loose dirt off his robes before letting him go.

Farin was tragically beautiful, which was one of the reasons Chardon felt others wanted to pick on him. He had stark black hair with slight golden colored waves in it and murky green eyes. Instead of fingernails, he had shiny black talons sharper than any cutting weapon. His full pink mouth that he inherited from Chardon completed the exotic features.

"They dared me to climb the big stone!" Farin's small voice attempted yelling. "My claws just slid on it and couldn't grip!"

He was disappointed, Chardon saw.

"Yes, well, next time they tease you, slice a piece of it off."

Trinon and Mota's posture went erect at such a suggestion.

"Let's not get all out of sorts over a little fun and games."

Mota raised a hand in protest.

Chardon sighed. "We are leaving soon and I don't want any incidents."

"Trinon is going to accompany him, so you need not worry." Mota turned back towards the way he came. "I'll see you off when the time comes. I have to tend to the other little ones."

He walked away and Chardon wondered how he got his personality. Neither of his parents were what one might call cheerful.

Chardon watched Modas wait in silence as she tended to a dirty Farin in the basin embedded in the chamber's floor. He didn't move an inch for the duration of the event but there was an expression on his face that Chardon did not like. How Modas felt towards Halfar was no secret. In her opinion that should not transfer to her child.

"Could you hand me a drying cloth?"

"As you wish."

Modas stepped further into the chamber, removed a cloth from its rack and handed it to Chardon. He never came any closer than required.

"Am I not worthy of your loyalty and protection any longer?"

"You will always have both."

"That's not why I asked, Modas." Chardon spat through gritted teeth.

"What is it you want from me?"

"Stop treating us like pariahs!"

"Understood."

Chardon slapped the wet cloth on the floor, startling both Farin and Modas, and turned to stare at Modas. Her eyes filled with tears.

"Does Modas not like Farin?" Farin asked softly, his eyes opened to their full extent.

Modas' eyes in turn grew wide with shock and obvious shame.

"I do like Farin, very much."

Farin, stark naked and not yet fully dry, smiled sweetly.

"I'll go prepare for the trip to Azrom," he said as he left the chamber.

In the hallway outside the chamber, Modas strode hurriedly towards the exit. At the end of the corridor he stopped, took a deep shaky breath and smashed his fist against the wall. His head hung down in despair. This was not how he envisioned Chardon's life. As her bodyguard, he should have prevented all that transpired from happening.

Raising his head, he looked up at the weak sun mocking him from above. If it were not for Halfar and his childish tantrum, they would still be on their home world.

And Chardon would be safe.

He would have gotten rid of Sestis easy enough in the beginning, before she had a foothold within the council.

Tiny laughter caught his ear and he cringed with pain. His little ones were playing in the fields further out and adjusting his vision saw Jaron, his mate and Chardon's cousin, playing with them. He loved her, he did. But, he wondered if things could have been different if he was not forbidden from who he wanted initially.

Would it have made me happy?

Modas straightened his posture and continued on to the council room for briefing regarding their departure. The selection of people the council chose to accompany Chardon was not to his liking. Trinon, was acceptable. Talas and Kelin he could do without. He had to deal with it because when it came to strategy Talas had no equal and he didn't go anywhere without Kelin.

Even more amazing was Jaron and Talas combining their talents lately. Modas sighed heavily. He had hoped to at least minimize Chardon's interactions with Halfar, mate or not.

Introductions

Halfar stood arms crossed with a look of anxiety and excitement all rolled into one. The gate was opening, signaling the arrival of Chardon's entourage from New Lassa. He would be able to hold his son, Farin, again. Of course, the boy would be a few years older now but he didn't care. A tight embrace from him was in Farin's near future. This new found emotion of fatherhood disturbed and amazed him. If he'd known how he would feel beforehand, he would have had more offspring. Surely Chardon would be willing to bear more for him.

Flanked on each side of him were his two generals, Rass and Kur. Halfar's cape, the color of human blood, sailed backwards revealing the black body armor underneath. Rass and Kur's were the color of azure sky. Behind them stood rows of royal guards in golden armor and red capes while the servants lined along the bridge wore thin robes. Fabrics in shades of bright reds, blues and gold swirled around in the wind created by the gate. The smell of freshly cleaned and oiled armor whiffed in the air.

The first to set foot on Azromian soil was Modas. He stood still at the threshold looking menacing with his six feet eight-inch frame and they both locked eyes. An unspoken resentment exchanged between them and Halfar knew instantly what the man beast's intentions were. He had anticipated this, and a plan was in place to thwart his every move if necessary.

Halfar could feel malicious intent coming from his right and snuck a glance at Rass whose expression was far from welcoming. Modas switched his gaze to Rass and gave a short nod.

Chardon came forth with Farin and Trinon. She was beautiful as always. Her white and gold robes flowed to the ground and as the sun caught her hair, turning it a deep golden color with streaks of dark red. An after effect of their combined DNA and Halfar approved of the change. His son's features surprised him.

How did I spawn such a beautiful creature?

He thought opening his arms wide for Farin, who ran joyously towards him.

"Well, I guess I will have to wait my turn then," Chardon sighed.

"I'm sure he has something else in store for you besides an embrace," Talas laughed softly from behind her.

His dirty blond hair fell in waves down the middle of his back resting on the reddish brown leather hide jacket. The color suited him so well, Chardon always wanted to ruin it.

Realizing he had not yet formally introduce anyone, Halfar shifted his son to the side and held out a hand to Chardon. As she came near, he grasped her hand and turned to the bridge. The guards parted in the center allowing entry. Hand in hand, they walked to the end and from the balcony, a sea of people could be seen assembled below. Groups of wattiors in caped battle armor with a few civilians mixed in waited patiently for their supreme ruler to speak. He had not released any information, so he knew this would be a shock.

"Victorious!" Halfar's voiced boomed in the air.

"Til death!" was the resounding reply from the masses and the guards behind him.

Chardon and the rest of her people appeared to be taken aback by the vocal assault. None of them had ever heard something so grand yet blood thirsty resound in the air as the Azromian race. She finally got to see why Halfar was called the Supreme Ruler.

"Though my absence has caused great unrest, I have returned with a new perspective," Halfar paused for a moment to make sure he had the right wording, "and a mate."

There was a loud gasp followed by silence.

"I present Chardon, the leader of Lassa," he paused again while ushering Chardon forward, "and the mother of my son, Farin." He turned the small boy around for all to see. The silence was deafening as Halfar waited for a response.

Then, an uproar of cheers.

General Kur stepped closer to him and whispered, "I believe you have just assured the security of our race, my lord." Kur returned to his position next to General Rass.

"Let the festival commence!" The captain of the royal guard commanded in a roar that sent the entire mob into a frenzy.

Halfar set Farin down and walked back towards the palace entrance with Chardon beside him. The royal guards closed ranks behind him and the Lassian entourage once the servants entered ahead to prepare service. He suddenly felt free of stress after decades of tension. Looking down, he saw Farin smiling brightly at him. His chest tightened with pride and affection.

Chardon made a mental map of the palace as she followed Halfar down the long hallway to his quarters. Farin clung to his father in silence having no interest in the scenery. The sound of their boots striking the hard floor echoed around them. In the distance, celebratory cheers continued to ring out.

The palace walls were sleek and shiny in a cream colored stone with dark markings swirled throughout it. Each panel was pristine and even the matching floors were devoid of residue one would see from foot traffic. Chardon wondered if they had been cleaned recently due their visit. Halfar must have wanted to make an impression.

As they passed personal chambers, Chardon realized there were no doors and no indication there ever had been. Each entrance was structure like a great hall or foyer. It unnerved her a bit since privacy had always been a standard. Halfar never mentioned the layout of the palace.

"Tell me," Chardon broke the eerie silence. "Why are there no doors?"

Halfar slowed his pace and looked upwards in thought.

"It was never an issue to bring up. We hide nothing." He glanced at her. "Are you concerned?"

"A little apprehensive, yes."

"Hmm." Halfar leaned close to her. "I think, you will find it a non-issue as well. Think of it as," he squinted, "that Earth word."

"Voyeurism?" Chardon's eyebrow arched upwards as she said it.

"Exactly."

"Were you always this perverse?"

Halfar stopped walking and a sheepish smile crossed his face.

"Perhaps."

Azrom's idea of festivities were grander than what Lassians were used to. The great hall was filled to the brim with royalty, guards and food. Talas seemed to be at ease, telling battle stories while Trinon grazed through the food along with Jaron. Chardon watched everyone in the room to get a feel for what was appropriate. She also did it to see who could be trusted.

Halfar clearly had no real affection for his royal bloodline.

Many of the royal family were arrogant, slovenly and had delusions of entitlement. They didn't seem to understand that Halfar could take it all away from them at any moment if he so chooses. A quick glance in Kelin's direction found him assessing the same thing.

"If I could do such a thing, I would have a long time ago," Halfar whispered in her ear. He seemed able to read her mind lately.

"Why can't you?" Chardon whispered back.

"My conscience won't let me do it. They are my blood relatives, and," he paused long enough to eat a small fruit, "not all of them are this bad."

Chardon gave him a dirty look and resumed her scan of the hall. One of the royal men caught her gaze. He smiled with malice and lust. His features were similar to Halfar's except his hair was shorter and dark blonde. Something about him made her feel uneasy. He suddenly blanched and turned away leaving Chardon confused until she turned to see Halfar's face.

"Still feel the same way?" Chardon chided him. Halfar's eyes darkened to a deep forest green. "Relax, my love," Chardon laughed. "I am not so easily swayed."

Halfar let out a loud sigh and did as instructed, relaxing onto the large cushion he was sitting on. Chardon reached over and stroked his hair. She stopped, realizing the hall had gone silent and everyone was staring at them. Looking down at Halfar, she saw his eyes were closed, enjoying the caress. In an instant she knew they had seen a weakness in their ruler and her body stiffened. Her people could feel it as well and they stood still waiting to strike if necessary.

A hand clamped onto her wrist, snapping her out of it. Halfar sat up and placed her hand in his. He had a look of acknowledgement and content. As his gaze fell on the occupants of the hall, an intense glow of red engulfed his pupils, making it known there was no opening to exploit his affections for Chardon. It even made Jaron turn pale. Chardon was reminded just how ruthless Halfar could be. He was, after all, the cause of Lassa's destruction.

Razznian Agenda

From space Planet Razzna appeared to be a ball of churning molten lava in shades of deep orange, red, brown and black. Its surface, dark and sinister, adding to the aesthetic with black rock covering the land as seas of red frothed along sandy deep russet brown beaches. Two moons glowed silver on the north side of the sky like eyes surveying the world for intruders.

Shores of black east of the red ocean shimmied revealing them to be giant ships sleek in structure yet somehow crude. Tiny red dots of light sprung to life along the sides of their hulls making them resemble an insect swarm. A slight humming resonated through the air sending vibrations along the surface. Small creatures camouflaged themselves with the environment as they scurried for cover.

On a craggy mountain sat large silver monuments that glistened like scales. The tops were daggers shooting upwards ending in tiny spikes. Sleek beetle ships hovered above while others rounded the perimeter in slow circulation. Light from the two moons made the structure glow unnaturally bright, almost blinding. The only majestic thing of beauty.

A group of twenty Razznians draped in deep brown hooded robes marched up the paved roadway towards the entrance of the shimmering compound. Included within their ranks was the spy returning from Earth. They all trekked in silence, tired from their journey. As low ranking warriors, they did not get to land their ship close to the base, and it had been an hour hike. Only higher ranked officers could use the transports. The trek was a lesson in humility.

One thought crossed their leader's mind on the way up.

Maybe we will be promoted for this information.

At the entrance, the entourage halted in front of fifty-foot-high double doors and waited for the guards on either side to usher them through. A second set of guards on the opposite side pulled the doors open halfway then stepped aside. The two guards waved the group in and as the last one entered the great hall, the doors were pushed shut creating a loud echo.

Everyone in the group removed their hoods out of respect for being in the same vicinity as their ruler. Eyes ranging from gold to blood red looked around before focusing their attention on the corridor that seemed nearly a mile long leading to a lift at the end. Heavy sighs were exhaled as they resigned themselves to the last leg of their journey.

On the lift they continued in silence as it went up, then sideways for quite a while and back to ascending until it slowed to a halt. The doors opened to another great hall except this time not five hundred feet from them sat their ruler on his throne. Dark red floor coverings ran from the lift to the throne in contrast with the shiny black marbled interior.

Advisors roamed around in black robes, the hoods red on the inside signifying their status. Servants were dressed similarly but the insides of their hoods were the same russet brown as the sands on the ocean beaches and their heads hung low in submission. The shuffling stopped and everyone's eyes landed on the entourage.

"We come with a report you may find interesting, my lord," the spy announced as his group bowed their heads to their ruler.

Lord Kraznan blinked his blood-red eyes and stopped fanning himself with the crude animal hide fabric rigid from chemical treatment. His black and golden colored scaled skin glinted from the hovering bulbs. He set down the fan and adjusted his black robe.

"Proceed." His guttural voice hissed across the hall.

"I have just come from a planet called Earth where Halfar was engaged in a battle with factions of his own enforcers. He seemed to be aiding the Earthlings."

"Intriguing. Continue."

"Halfar's armada and the Earthlings were being assisted by manbeasts and energy wielders."

This made Lord Kraznan sit up straight.

"From where?" he demanded.

"It seems, not all of the Lassians were destroyed. Halfar kept some of them and those who survived have relocated."

Lord Kraznan's eyes grew wide. The deal between himself and the Lassian female leader bequeathed the Lassian race to the Razznians for slavery. Also, a foothold inside planet Azrom's political engine to ultimately bring it down. Sestis would have been made ambassador to a number of planets Razzna held under their thumb.

It was all contingent on Planet Lassa being conquered and in league with Azrom. With the destruction of Lassa and Halfar's unexpected flight from Azrom, the deal was not enforced. But now, knowing there were survivors, he could still enslave them. Their abilities would be perfect for manual labor.

"This is most excellent. Your Nest will be promoted." He saw the gleam in their eyes. "For your next mission, you will find out where the Lassians are. You may have to infiltrate Azrom to do so. Are you prepared?"

"Of course, your grace," the group's leader bowed.

"We will depart immediately."

"Good. You may move your ship and dock at the main hub to replenish supplies."

As the group left, Lord Kraznan leaned further back into his throne and sat in reverie. Across the five solar systems in their universe, Razznians were considered one of the most feared. It wasn't because of their might but more so their level of ruthlessness. Some have said they even rivaled Planet Azrom during certain time periods.

It may turn out to be a great new era for his species yet. Manual labor was causing undue hardship on the lower ranks after the collapse of their automated drones nearly a century ago. Especially since the manufacturers refused to honor the warranties when fighting broke out between the two races. Having strong manbeasts would alleviate the burden until a new resolution was developed. That female Lassian creature Sestis' proposal would have been a gift.

Sestis

Air condensed and began to swirl, forming a spiral that grew darker until turning a deep purplish black. Pulsing like a pool of liquid it collapsed into itself revealing a tunnel of stars. Light shot forth and as it diminished, a small entourage of five were left in its place at the portal entrance on Planet Razzna.

Sestis, the mate of Chardon, leader of Planet Lassa, took one look at the terrain and grimaced. Her impression of the Razznians was low already, and this did not help any. The four body guards accompanying her were already on alert in case Lord Kraznan's sudden invitation was a trap. His interest in her agendas struck a suspicion within her but at the same time, intrigue. This may be a great opportunity in her favor.

Squinting to adjust her eyesight, a figure in a long hooded robe stood at the control panel. She took note of the scaly skin and glint of red eyes focused on the console. Behind him stood a small horde of Razznians, all hooded, waiting in silence. As Sestis and her entourage approached, the horde surrounded them. Their movements served to guide the visitors towards the only thing on the planet that could be seen even from space; the royal palace. At the palace entrance, Sestis smirked at the gigantic doors.

How ridiculous.

They were reptilian, not giant beasts. The inner transport system made her laugh as well. Her escorts frown in unison at the sound. Once the doors opened to the throne room, Sestis had to muster all her sanity not to burst into a guffaw. She could feel her guards stiffen behind her.

The throne room was a humid, dimly lit hall swarming with lazy Razznians in silken robes being serviced by hooded subordinates. Sestis caught a whiff of something that reminded her of spoiled vegetation. She instinctively raised the back of one hand and discreetly covered her nose. Behind the hanging sleeves, she spoke.

"Lord Kraznan, greetings from Lassa." She bowed her head slightly.

The barrel chested ruler sat fully on the throne, legs spread wide eagled. His thick tail lay directly in between, the tip hitting the floor. The visual was disgusting and she assumed to know why he did it.

You wish you had genitalia so supreme.

She snickered to herself despite her surroundings. His eyes laid on her and he sat up with what must have been some form of a smile. She couldn't tell because his mouth was two thin lines. Her assumption proved correct when a row of sharp teeth were revealed.

"Lady Sestis, how good of you to accept my invitation."

"It was quite a surprise, thank you."

"To have something so lovely grace our presence," Lord Kraznan sat up, "Is an honor."

Sestis removed her hand from her mouth and smiled sweetly.

"The pleasure is all mine, I hope."

Her insides tensed and she felt the meal she consumed beforehand curdle at the thought of him touching her in that way most of the other male delegates did when they were alone with her. She only allowed it to gain a rapport with them, and some sense of trust, but did not enjoy.

"Please, come." He motioned to a doorway off in the back corner to her left. "We can discuss ideas privately." His eyes roamed her entourage. "Unless you do not feel comfortable."

"I think privately would be best." She glanced back at her guards. "Remain here."

Sestis followed the ruler into the secondary room making sure not to accidentally step on his dragging tail. It was tempting to do so even knowing how cruel that would be. His crimson robes with gold overlay made him appear more majestic as they flowed around him. She had never really been this close to the ruler and now saw how tall he was in comparison to his subjects. He stood above her though not by much.

At nearly 184cm tall, Sestis was by no means someone to take lightly. She was the same height as her mate, Chardon, and interpreted this as being on equal footing. Even her guards were intimidated by her but she was sure it may have to do with more than just her size.

She reached behind her neck and pulled her golden auburn hair forward from the constraints of her high collared cape. The thick waves fell down passed her shoulders and covered the front of her dress, hiding her cleavage. Lord Kraznan had peeked over and seemed disappointed. She kept the small smile on her face.

"So, Lord Kraznan, to what do I owe this unexpected gesture?"

Sestis sat down on an oversized plush in the middle of the room. The ruler wasted no time in joining her, his breath brushing her neck making the hairs stand on end.

"It has come to my attention that you have a rather," he paused for the right word, "anathema for the manbeasts of your race." His split tongue slipped out and ran across his lips before going back through the slits of his mouth.

Sestis shuddered inwardly.

"They are great warriors, I will admit that, but nothing so special as to rely on them for our protection. We have our own powers just as deadly."

She smiled as she said it to emphasize not to underestimate her but it did not deter him in the least for his tongue ran across her cheek, his eyes fluttered in ecstasy.

"Yesss…you are very capable of handling yourself."

Sestis playfully pushed him away with a sly smile on her face, hiding how nauseous she felt. Every male species she encountered wanted to touch or taste her flesh regardless of permission despite her imperative to keep them focused on her agenda.

Plan of Action

A general assembly of military power along with the Lassians created a war council to plan battle strategies against the Razznians. After a few years, they were still not in agreement on how to proceed. Battle was another five years away which irritated Halfar. Between his Generals' ideas and that of the Lassians, plans were at opposite ends of the spectrum: Defend or deploy. He liked neither option. The last thing he wanted to do was go into Razznian territory. On the other hand, he didn't want to sit and wait for them to attack Azrom. He wanted no civilian casualties after the last long war that left his people nearly devastated.

Sars stood at the helm of his newly equipped battle cruiser with newfound determination. No longer just a low level Razznian spy, he relished in the chance to prove his worth. A small band of loyal soldiers he chose were part of his crew and he felt the same loyalty to them. The last mission found them on that dreadful planet called Earth and it left much to be desired. Now they headed for planet Azrom, home to Halfar and his deadly Armada. Right into the lion's mouth. Sneaking onto its surface was not for the faint of heart. Sars, of course, had a plan.

Getting caught was part of an option if necessary. The thought of General Rass, or Kur, capturing his men made his scales tingle in fear. A small ting sounded to signal the ship was in proximity of Azrom's orbit. He turned to his navigator seated below him.

"Once we are in position behind the second moon, cloak the ship and stand by." He was answered with a nod. To his second in command standing next to him, he announced, "Prepare the pod suits. We will descend from the far side."

"Of course, sir. The drop will be taxing in the free fall, and it will be quick."

"That is the idea."

"Make sure the thrusters are reversed at least one kilometer before impact."

"Understood."

"Sir, if I may say, this is an audacious plan."

"Exactly. They would never suspect such a bold move."

"Good hunting, sir." His second in command bowed slightly as Sars left the bridge.

A smile crept on Sars' face as he strode down the corridor. Success without risk was not his idea of a great mission. He was the only one who volunteered for the previous and reaped the reward, apparently having a skillset for infiltration. Slowing to a stop in front of the lift, he waved one hand across the panel to open it. After allowing him in, the lift doors closed automatically and shot downwards to the equipment hold on the lower level. He reached his destination in less than three seconds.

The doors opened to a din of activity as eleven Razznians slithered about checking their weapons and body suits for any defects. This group of soldiers he trusted above all others. They had been with him from inception into the militia not long after being hatched from different nests on the same day. Each was like a sibling to him; his own throng.

One of them halted his own preparations to hand Sars his gear before resuming protocol. Sars began his inspection of the pack making sure to go over his equipment twice. When everyone had donned on all the necessary wares, he hit the indicator on the side of the door to open the first airlock. They all filed into the secondary chamber and he could feel their anticipation.

Along the walls were twelve pod suits ready for pilots. They had been specifically designed for this mission and tested only twice before being handed over to Sars. He made his request for their creation as a necessity for the success of the mission. Absentmindedly caressing one nearest to him he was shocked and delighted they were approved.

The podsuits were like personalized drop ships in the form of reinforced body armor able to withstand atmospheric entry. Each unit was fully enclosed, protecting its pilot from the intense heat and possible hard landings. Although, if it went crashing down too fast, the body inside would liquefy on impact. Hence, the timing of the thrusters per his second in command's instructions.

"Approaching drop point." The feminine voice boomed from the internal communicators throughout the ship.

Sars, along with his group, strapped themselves into the pod suits and sealed them with the touch of a button located on the left shoulder. Inside the suits, holoscreens lit up displaying the control module for navigation. Tiny connectors spread out along each soldier's body, tapping into their muscles to allow maneuverability. The pod suits were piloted based on the occupant's body movements.

The airlock hissed as all the air was removed and the chamber rotated to lock onto the outer door. A loud click signaled they were in position and the chamber tilted so that their heads pointed out towards the door. On the other side, space waited for their arrival.

"Opening outer lift." The voice announced.

As the door eased open, sucking the air out of the chamber, Sars braced himself even though he knew it would do him no good. He saw the edge of the second moon and just beyond it, planet Azrom seeming so close he felt he could touch them.

"Releasing pods."

One by one, each pod was disconnected from the chamber and projected into the darkness of space at speeds the soldiers had never experienced. The free fall intensified and Sars' watched the distance meter inside his helmet for the correct timing.

"Close your helmet shutters!" He commanded, his voice shaky from the descent. When he saw all the face plates on the pods go black, he did the same. "Activate thrusters!" His teeth clenched down hard as the pod suits barreled mercilessly into Azrom's stratosphere.

"Ahh!" Farin yelled with excitement as he climbed onto the balcony's ledge and pointed up to the sky, eyes wide. "Shooting stars!"

Trinon was on the ground resting with his back against the railings and had to turn his head to see what Farin was going on about. Manbeasts had superior sight and his eyes zeroed in on the glowing objects. Even with the after burn blazing around them he could tell they were not what Farin claimed.

Shooting stars my eye.

He stood up and grabbed Farin under the arms from behind, lifting him off the ledge.

No longer small and demure, Farin was heavy. Trinon had to put more muscle into lifting him. At five feet tall, the half Azromian half Lassian was even more stunningly beautiful. His shiny black talons were longer and deadlier.

Trinon made sure to keep clear of them.

"Time to go in."

"But, I want to see the rest of the stars." Farin whined as Trinon set him down onto the platform.

"I know, but we'll be late for evening meal."

"Okay!" Farin smiled up at him.

Trinon glanced back once more as the last object headed for the planet's surface. He frowned.

Has it already begun?

A firm battle plan was not even in effect yet.

Soft light, emitted from the large holoscreen set in the center of room on a raised platform, spread across the observation chamber, casting an eerie glow on the faces surrounding it. General Rass, Kur, Modas and Trinon stood in a semicircle watching, in silence, the transmitted images of the tiny fireballs falling out of the sky then crashing to the sur- face. As it progressed, Kur arched an eyebrow in amusement while Rass' eyes went wide in disbelief.

"How bold." Kur broke the mood.

"We need to know who they are."

Rass leaned further down, attempting to identify the objects.

"Can you not tell from the characteristics of the ships?" Trinon asked as he too leaned down, setting his forearms flat on the console.

"I have never seen anything like them." Rass responded.

Two royal guards entered the chamber and bowed to the Generals. The first to stand back upright spoke. "Generals, we have pinpointed the sector of impact. Shall we inform our ruler and send out the scouts?"

Both Rass and Kur slid their eyes towards him and the looks left him feeling cold inside, and afraid. The other guard took a small step back creating the right amount of distance between them just in case.

"No," Rass answered, turning his attention back to the holoscreen. "There is no need for Halfar to know of this at this junction. We are his Generals. It would be a disgrace if we could not handle something as trivial as infiltration."

"No need to worry. Whoever they are, they will not make it off this planet alive," Kur interjected as he focused on the looped transmission.

"Or intact," Rass included.

"How clever." Kur tapped the screen and the image froze. "Now, what shall we do about this, hmm?" Everyone in the room stared at it in confusion until they all saw it. "They have split into three groups."

"Yes, one group is on the outer rim of the city and the other two are on the far side." Rass tapped on the objects near the outer rim. "There is only one reason to land so far into the wastelands outside the perimeter."

"All roads lead to the palace. They are going to have to find a way to hide amongst the merchants of the market square in the town that sits on the outskirts."

"Send out four scout units. We will surround and observe them for the moment." Rass instructed the two guards.

Kur fixed his gaze on Modas and Trinon.

"Let's not cause any ripples, shall we?" Modas nodded in response. "I do not have to ask that Farin be protected now more than ever."

"Done!"

Trinon slapped his hands on the console, causing the image to shake wildly before it corrected itself.

Rass and Kur glanced at each other as the two guards, along with Modas and Trinon, exited the chamber.

The same thought ran in their minds.
This was going to be thrilling.

Sars surveyed the area his team had landed in while they activated the camouflage on the pod suits. The sky was devoid of clouds making the sun too bright for his reptilian eyes. Powdery beige colored dirt covered the ground forming whirlwinds of dust every time his feet moved along it. Some of the scarce trees appeared dead or dying. There was nothing for as far as the eye could see except for a small community off in the distance. Farther away stood the palace, looming majestic and menacing.

So, this is Azrom.

He expected a better environment. Then he remembered Halfar was a tyrant who ruled with an iron fist.

"Let's get going. It will take about four days to get to that village. Once there we can plan how to get to the palace." His crew nodded in unison.

"This place…this planet," One of his men began. "It's desolate."

"Mmm hmm. I know." Sars responded.

They all donned long hooded robes and began their march through the Azrom desert towards the royal palace. Sars knew their entry would be obvious by now and had mentally prepared his team and himself for the inevitable fight that might occur. He hoped the other two teams had landed safely and were also headed towards the palace. His orders were complete radio silence until they reached their destination.

Trinon found Talas lounging on the ledge of a balcony with a tiny smirk on his face. His arms supported his weight as he leaned back, one leg hanging over and the other propped under him. A small breeze ruffled his blonde tresses, now nearly twice as long as before.

He sighed, tilting his head towards Trinon and opened his eyes.

"Sneaking up on me?"

"That's kind of impossible," Trinon replied as he stood next to him and leaned on the ledge. He took in the view of the land before him and frowned.

"Halfar does not treat his people very well, does he? They may be of one race but I see poverty, discrimination and food depletion," Talas said.

"How are you so observant? I can see for miles and didn't know all of that."

"It's not about what you see, but how you perceive what you see." Talas looked up at the sky. "I think he means well. He just doesn't know how to rule."

"This from the person who got duped by Sestis and opened the gate for a planet bomb?"

"Ouch!" Talas feigned injury. "Was that really necessary?"

Trinon glanced at him, quickly changing the subject.

"Did you hear about the shooting stars?"

"Oh, yes. The enemy is bringing the battle here and for obvious reasons."

"You know why?"

Trinon straightened his posture and stared at Talas in awe.

"Trinon, I am a strategist above all else and even those two Generals would have figured it out as well." He swung his legs over the ledge and set himself down on the balcony. "Why have you sought me out this time?"

"Can we have a practice session?"

Trinon's eyes filled with anticipation.

"You know your father does not approve of you

learning new fighting skills from anyone who is not a manbeast."

"He's too full of pride to learn new things, but I am a new generation of manbeast."

"That you are." Talas stretched his body, inhaling, then let out a deep breath. "Fine. Find a good spot then."

"I already did," Trinon smiled mischievously

The great hall was filled to capacity with Azrom advisors, both military and political, along with the Lassians. Tension ran high as each member sized up the other in intimidation. Lassa was seen as an inferior power on the scale of interstellar battle not an enemy. Chardon knew going in from when he visited the other worlds as a representative. It was the equivalent of being spit on. He could feel Halfar on edge by his side and not just for this reason. Chardon had chosen to attend the meeting as a male to show strength and authority. Halfar thought it unnecessary, even antagonizing.

Chardon took note of the clash in attire from each race. The Azromians were identical with the only variation being the colors to define ranks and status. His people were a mish mash of different styles, none defining them as the powerful fighters they were, nor what planet they hailed from. Chardon forced himself not to frown. That being known, he felt no need to militarize his race to such an extent. Individuality is what made them Lassian.

Halfar repositioned himself on the gold colored throne with one foot set on its edge so he could rest an elbow on his knee. He was the only one in the room sitting. To his right stood Kur and Rass in full regalia looking bored. To Chardon's left was Modas, Talas and Jaron. The hall seemed to be split down the middle with both races apart from each other on either side like a great river.

"Status!" Halfar yelled, startling everyone out of their staring contests.

Azrom and Lassa's head councilman took a quick glare at each other and the Azromian stepped forward, his head held high in defiance.

"It has been confirmed, my Lord. The Razznians have gathered a battle fleet and are on the move. It seems they have mapped an unusual route to get to our system. A smaller fleet is lying in wait facing the opposite direction."

He smiled as he turned to the Lassian councilman.

"This also confirms our previous assessment." The Lassian began. "The second fleet is waiting for Azrom to open the pathway to Lassa. It was always their agenda to take over and enslave our race per Sestis' deal with them. They obviously underestimate us." He too smiled wide glancing over at the Azrom councilman.

"I find it strange," another Azrom advisor interjected. "Why would their fleet advance on our system? No race has dared outright attack us since the Utalizar war. Being the Razznians are normally not aggressors, would they be so bold as to come here?"

Kur and Rass quickly glanced at each other with knowing looks then reverted their attention back to the councilmen. Chardon narrowed his eyes, not able to stop the feeling of dread and betrayal in his gut. Halfar hadn't noticed his two Generals' interaction. Chardon wondered if he already knew something or was totally indifferent to what his military was up to.

"If I may," Chardon spoke.

The hall went deathly quiet. Halfar, Rass and Kur slowly turned to stare at him in disbelief.

"Since the Razznians have grown so bold as to target both planets, maybe we could cross train our fighters to maximize our success."

Only the sound of a light breeze flowing through the hall could be heard. A dense atmosphere churned about and the faces of the people on the floor below changed into something sinister.

"Train?" Azrom's head military councilman barked. "What could we possibly learn from these...?" He stopped short.

"And why should we let them know our battle techniques? They may try to use them against us in the near future," another councilman added.

"As if that would work. We will always be superior," said another Azromian.

A loud din filled the room and weapons were drawn when the sound of claws echoed throughout from the Lassian manbeasts preparing for a fight. Chardon pursed his lips in frustration. This was stupidity on both sides.

"Enough!" Halfar commanded.

Weapons were sheathed, and claws detracted. Everyone's attention went to the supreme ruler sitting upright, his knuckles white on the arms of the throne. His eyes had turned a brilliant green and burned with dis- gust. Chardon looked away, also afraid of that stare.

"Is victory not our goal?" He asked sharply.

"Why, yes, my Lord." The Azrom councilman replied in a shaky tone.

"Then what is the problem?" He turned his head towards the man- beasts lined up on the left side of the hall. "When you underestimate an entire race, what happens?"

"Defeat," the councilman answered softly. "What happens?" Halfar yelled.

"Defeat!" The councilman cried out.

"These manbeasts are just as strong as us. Learning new fighting techniques benefits all."

"It is quite an audacious proposal," the Lassian councilman announced. "Though our manbeasts are a little leery about teaching outside their race and vice versa."

Chardon saw a look of defiance on Modas face and knew it was going to be an uphill battle. Trinon, on the other hand looked excited and glanced over at Talas with some sort of anticipation. It must have been on their minds as well. Chardon thought to himself.

"As for battle plans," Halfar continued. "We need to know their trajectories in full to either deter or annihilate successfully. Get to it." Halfar addressed the last to Kur and Rass as he rose from his throne, stepping down onto the blood red carpet that made a trail across the room all the way to the doors. He held out a hand and Chardon took it.

They exited the great hall together in silence until they reached the end of the balcony where Halfar stopped. He turned to face him then grabbed Chardon by the shoulders and squeezed.

"That was dangerous!" He hissed softly, peeking around the corner to make sure his guards were not in earshot.

"But necessary to ensure the survival of both planets."

"I know that, you know that. It's not about the right thing to do, it's about pride!"

"That's…!" Chardon started to yell.

"Stupid," Halfar said softly, letting his arms drop. "My race. We've been through a lot and are very possessive of certain things."

"That's obvious. Now, how do we get both our races to cooperate?"

✳

General Kur strolled down the walkway that ran along the quarters outside. The tip of his long saber nearly touched the ground as it hung low from his side. He stared at the white stone under his feet as he walked in a haze of confusion. Something stirred in him and he was frustrated due to not being able to identify it. A tress of his dark forest green hair fell across one shoulder and he glanced at it as if it were an intruder. It made him realize just how irritated he had become over the tiniest things since coming home.

At the entrance of a personal chamber he stopped mid stride. His back foot sat arched upward on its tip. Not knowing where he was, he raised his head and turned, curious as to what lay inside. The late day sun made it hard to see in the dark room, so he waited for his eyes to adjust. As they did, he saw the sleeping figure on the bed stir and raise up.

Rass used one hand to push himself up from under the coverings and the other to shield his eyes from the sunlight. His dark hair had grown down to his waist and wrapped around him like tendrils. Kur pivoted to stand facing him from the entryway.

A burning sensation filled his eyes as he advanced into the chamber, shedding saber and clothes as he got closer to the bed. Rass did not seem surprised, not moving even when Kur threw off the coverings revealing that Rass was sleeping naked in female form as he climbed on.

"I'm tired." Rass said in a defeated tone.

"I know." Kur reached around her waist and turned her over. His body covered hers and grabbing the edge of a tossed cover flung it over them. "I need you."

Rass placed her hands on his cheeks and they stared into each other's eyes. They didn't break contact as Kur entered her roughly. It had been too long, and he knew he could not be gentle even if he tried. No, Rass would have to endure his animalistic love making. He could hear no sounds as he watched her mouth forming in cries with her eyes closed tight.

Why had I tuned everything out? He asked himself.

Shaking his head to clear the fuzziness, he repositioned his body and put some of his weight on his arms as he placed them above on the wall.

Sound returned and the scream filling his ears let him know he was in fact hurting her. He abruptly stopped, looking down at Rass' sweat drenched body, his own sweat dripping onto hers. A sense of dread came over him. The sun was setting. How long have I been here? Rass' breathing slowed, and he could feel the pulse of her body still going quite fast. Kur removed one hand from the wall and stroked her lips before kissing them.

Relieved that he had not caused any damage, he resumed his thrusts, this time a little less aggressively. He could hear her cries of pleasure and pain which heightened his lust. As he released his seed into her, he finally understood what had been eating away at him; desire. Euphoria swept over him as he buried his head in the crook of Rass' neck.

"Better?" Rass whispered softly in a hoarse voice.

Kur kissed her and rolled over, taking her with him so that she lay on top of him. He watched her fall into a deep sleep within moments, and he followed not long after. The last time he had ever been satisfied was with Rass, and that was nearly half a century ago.

Halfar stood leaning against the rails directly across from Rass' chamber watching his two Generals reconnect after so many decades. He had also been walking along in thought when he noticed Kur's mindless stroll. Curious, he had followed. With his elbows resting on the ledge, hands dangling, he cocked his head to one side and observed Kur's animal descent into brutal sex.

How childish.

A twinge of jealously crept in and Halfar knew where it came from. Seeing them made him wonder if they were still capable of leading his Armada.

We shall see.

Pushing off the ledge, Halfar stood up and walked back down the walkway to the main palace sector. It was getting dark and his advisors were waiting.

TWO:

Not a United Front

One thing Modas did not tolerate was the meddling in the affairs of Manbeasts. He felt that his kind had survived all this time due to their strict policy of only handing down their fighting techniques to their own. The Azromians seemed to concur because there was a perpetual stalemate in the battle arena located near the main palace. It wasn't just them. Modas had no intention of teaching his fellow Lassians either and that put a great deal of tension on everyone in the area.

He could see Talas leering at him and knew what the sword wielder was thinking. Even Chardon had suggested that his way was outdated. An invisible line had been drawn in the white sand of the arena floor. No one budged. Both races stood in a single file line across from each other, unhappy with the turn of events.

"How about a short demonstration of fighting skills to clear the air?" General Kur suggested sweetly. "Relieve some tension, maybe?" He sat in the royal pit high above the field in full battle armor looking down on them with contempt.

Modas asked himself for the hundredth time why that creature was allowed to live. The whole plan centered on the General's demise, yet Chardon demanded he be saved. Kur's suggestion was not warranted because Modas had that in mind anyway. He had gone head to head with the mutated enforcers Kur had created.

Never against a true Azrom warrior.

"Agreed," he replied and heard a snort come from Talas at the other end of the line.

"It seems Talas does not approve?" Kur inquired.

"I suppose, my weak and inferior warriors should go sit in the stands and watch the real fighters go at."

Talas nodded towards the seating areas and the Lassian warriors broke rank to follow him across the field, leaving just the Manbeasts.

The Azrom Commander turned red.

"Are you mocking us?" He yelled, stepping forward with his one arm already forming a giant claw.

Modas stiffened, not expecting a backlash from Talas' judgment to let him handle the demonstration. Without looking back, he could feel Talas' entourage halt at the accusation. There was no need to have the Lassian warriors fight since his race of manbeasts were the better fighters. He didn't understand what the issue was.

"On the contrary, Commander," Talas replied turning his head slightly. "I just think we should wait our turn. Can't have two races against one, isn't that right General?"

Kur's lips curved into something that wasn't a smile.

"Funny. That is exactly what occurred on Earth, if I remember correctly." Talas shrugged, raising his hands up. "Very well, the Manbeasts will go up against the elite enforcers commanded by Yokun." The Azrom Commander bowed. "And the Lassian warriors will go up against one of the main battalion squads."

"Why would you do that?" Modas demanded.

"Beast against beast, man against man. That's only fair, correct?"

Kur leaned back from the balcony and sat down in the white stone seat behind him.

The squadron of soldiers left the field towards the opposite side of Talas' group and once both sides were seated, Modas surveyed the field. Twelve elites were in front of his seven manbeasts. He liked the odds and to acknowledge so, his claws grew out signaling his warriors to do the same.

"Let the demonstration begin!" Kur cried out with joy as Halfar and Chardon arrived to see the first clash.

One by one, Azrom's elite shifted into their monstrous forms. Grappling claws, scorpion like tails and hard-shelled bodies stood ready for a fight against the flesh and bone of Manbeasts. Each side emitted battle cries of ear piercing decibels and the sounds of their bodies colliding was that of a slaughter house. Blood flowed instantly.

Modas was matched with the commander and was surprised to find himself barely keeping up. The commander had claws that of an Earth lobster, like Halfar. With deadly swipes coming at him full speed, Modas was only able to dodge two or three. He dropped low and swung one leg to topple the commander. In the split second before it connected, the creature shot upwards.

Before Modas could move, the commander was inches from him, claws open ready to snap shut around his neck. Calling upon every muscle in his body, he was able to avoid a beheading. A fairly deep cut appeared along his clavicle. The speed of his movement sent him across the arena, still in a crouched position, raising a tidal wave of white sand on each side of him. He stopped at three quarters the length of arena.

Out of the corner of his eye he saw Talas raise an eyebrow, a tiny smile on his face. Talas then tilted his head towards the middle of the field. As Modas turned he saw a flash of color coming at him and immediately jumped to his right. To his amazement, the blur corrected its advance making a beeline to him. With nowhere else to go, Modas made a bold decision and laid flat on the ground just as the commander got within a few meters. The commander, with no time to correct his direction, went crashing into the wall behind him.

Thinking it was safe to stand up, Modas began to push himself off the ground until he noticed movement in the cloud of debris near the wall. He was knocked backward and before he could slide any further from the commander, claws grabbed hold of his robes and yanked him back to rest under the commander's other claw ready to strike.

As it came down, the commander disappeared and was replaced by two leather clad legs standing above him. The gust of wind that had accompanied them died and a long split-back cloak fell over the legs. Between them, Modas saw the commander out cold against another section of the wall, the impact leaving a large chunk of it falling to the ground.

"Losing your touch, old man?" Trinon turned his head back to look down on him.

Modas noticed that there was not a cut or scrape on his son meaning the blood splatter on his cloak and tunic was not his. The cocky smile made him a little angry, mostly proud. Heavy silence caught his ears and he looked around to see the fighting had halted. Everyone seemed to be in awe of Trinon and his Manbeasts seemed confused. Trinon stepped to one side and held out his hand. Modas clasped it and let himself be pulled up. In the seating area, Talas looked proud, and nervous at the same time.

"What's going on? Why have we stopped?"

From above Halfar leaned over the balcony ledge.

"I believe that is enough for today. Please have your wounds tended to and freshen up. There are still a few hours before evening meal, so rest."

He left the royal pit along with Chardon and Kur.

"What just happened, Trinon?" Modas stared at him. "What did you do?" His eyes narrowed as his son's eyes rolled upward and the tip of his tongue peeked out from the corner of his lips.

"I saved your honor?" Trinon replied.

"That's not…!" Modas began.

"Come now." Talas jumped down from the seating area onto the field. "Gladly take your lumps and thank your son," he said playfully.

Modas took another glance around the arena and saw the white sand stained with different shades of blood. He had been too confident in the strength of his Manbeasts and this was the result. During all the decades of touring for the council, Lassian and Azromian warriors had never fought each other. They did see the other's battles from afar.

We must be stronger.

Everyone exited the arena not talking or looking at each other. It was better that way. Of all the warriors who fought, Trinon was the only one who strode out with his hands clasped behind his head and a stupid grin.

What did I miss?

Modas was irritated.

On the platform in the middle of Halfar's meeting chamber Chardon plopped down onto a giant cushion set. Shallow bowls of Azrom flowers in various colors were in each corner. Four more cushions arranged strategically around him awaited their patrons. He leaned back and stared up at the ceiling as he replayed the battle 'demonstration' in his mind. Seeing Modas struggle was a surprise and knew it was based on the Manbeast's own miscalculations.

And then there was Trinon who ended it all.

Loud clanking boots striking the floor broke Chardon's thoughts, Halfar entered the chamber followed by Kur and Talas. As they stepped up onto the platform, also settling down in a giant cushion, servants flowed out of the corners with carafes of cool drink and platters of local fruit. They set them in the center of the platform and left just as stealthily as they came out.

Talas sat legs apart resting his arms on his knees. His head hung low between them, his hair brushing the floor. Kur filled a clear flute from one of the carafes and took a sip before leaning back. Halfar stretched out and crossed his legs and arms while staring upwards. No one spoke for what seemed like minutes.

"Chardon?" Halfar began and turned his head to meet his gaze. "What was that? I have seen manbeasts fight on several occasions although nothing like how young Trinon moved."

"I have an idea," Chardon replied.

"I know for a fact you nor Jaron fight like that either."

Kur raised an eyebrow and took another sip of his drink.

"I believe we have never seen an actually Lassian warrior fight, isn't that so, Chardon?"

"That would be correct."

"You were always surrounded by manbeasts or energy users when you traveled, never a warrior. We assumed they were inferior and knowing the fighting technique of manbeasts up close, I say Trinon has learned something new from one of them." He glanced over at Talas along with Chardon and Halfar. "It seems we wholly underestimated the Lassian race, my lord."

"Talas." Chardon called to him. When there was no reply, he tried again. "Talas!"

Talas' head shot up and he came into the gaze of all

three who sat in his line of sight. His dirty blonde hair went flying backwards in disarray framing his face. A look of shock and confusion greeted them.

"You always told me that you could never compete with a manbeast and all of Lassa believes this."

"Yes."

"Talas." Chardon said his name through gritted teeth.

"I lied." Talas managed a tiny smile and it immediately disappeared.

"What exactly is his title, Chardon?" Halfar inquired.

"He is the leader of our warriors. We don't really have titles."

"So," Kur leaned forward. "The backstabbing, incompetent Talas is actually a true Lassian warrior. Tell me, Talas, is all the lacking a ruse?"

"Pretty much." Talas nodded.

"He is also our strategist along with Jaron, as you know." Chardon added.

"In that case, tell us how to get our races to cooperate." Halfar said.

Talas shook his head and reached into the platter for a small fruit the size of a lemon. He tossed it up in the air a couple of times and then took a bite. After chewing it all and swallowing he replied.

"If I only knew how." Talas took another bite. "Modas won't like this."

"Indeed." Kur leaned back from him as he responded.

The bathing chamber reserved for the manbeasts was larger than any they had ever encountered. Seven of the ten wide basins set deep in the floor and were filled with lightly scented frothing liquid. Glow orbs hovered over them giving some ambience. An attendant sat on the edge of each one waiting for their charge.

Modas and his manbeasts stood at the entryway in hesitation, not ready or willing to strip down and let a stranger scrub them down. All except Trinon, whose lips formed a wide grin before he stripped naked and hurried towards the fourth basin down. He slid into it slowly and made a loud sigh. As he spread his arms across the edge of the tub, leaning his head back, the attendant grabbed a scrubbing sponge from the tray and stepped in with him.

"Better hurry, Father. The water doesn't stay hot forever."

Manbeasts glanced nervously around at each other then Modas. Cautiously, they moved towards the open basins and began to remove their blood-stained gear. Modas was the last to step forward and stopped at the empty basin with a male attendant sitting patiently for him. Without looking at anyone, he slowly removed his robes and boots, letting them drop onto the floor. He entered the water and sat on the bench along the inside. Perfectly still, he waited for the attendant who came in sponge in hand to scrub him.

"Oh, Father!" Trinon burst out laughing. "See reason."

Modas glanced over at his son and remained unmoving as the attendant raised his arm and began cleaning. A feeling of humiliation came even as he knew there was nothing to be done about the bathing or the battle as well. The sponge went past his line of sight and was now on his chest. Jaron was the only other being who had ever touched him while naked. He resisted his urge to slap the man's hand away knowing it would be an insult.

A female attendant came around to the other side of his basin and poured in a light-colored powder. As she left, Modas felt the tension in his body start to unwind. She went to all the others, doing the same.

Before his eyes closed, his body slumped against the

ledge, he could hear Trinon laughing in delight.

"How was your bath? It was refreshing, I hope." Halfar's head advisor asked as the manbeasts crossed the threshold of the same banquet chamber where Halfar's feast for Chardon took place.

"Intriguing." Modas replied.

"Invigorating!" Trinon added.

"Excellent."

The advisor turned from them and went to sit at the table along the far wall closest to the one reserved for Halfar and his group. He gestured to a table opposite his where the Azrom commander and his elite were seated.

"Commander," Modas nodded to him.

"Lassian," The commander spat.

"I will not tolerate any of that!"

Halfar burst into the room from the far left, followed by his generals and Chardon.

Every Azrom soldier stood up and bowed, yelling, "My Lord!"

Seeing that none of the Lassians did the same, looks of disdain fell upon them.

Halfar was about to make another outburst. Chardon, in female form per his earlier request stopped him. She pointed to Talas sitting at the other table with the Lassian warriors.

"He is neither our lord nor master, thus, we do not bow to him in submission. We will however bow to his allegiance." Talas stood and all the Lassians, including manbeasts, followed suit. They made a bow and returned to sitting. The Azromians did the same.

From the right entrance Trinon came out with Farin and led him to Chardon before going to sit with the rest of the manbeasts. The Azromians sat admiring the little one as he climbed on Halfar's lap when he sat down. His smile was enchanting.

"Father, did you see the shooting stars last moon?"

A great heavy silence filled the room and Trinon covered his face with one hand while Kur turned slowly towards the child in disbelief. Halfar's lips twitched until curving into a smile.

"No, my son, I did not. What kind of shooting stars?"

"They were different colors and it was daylight."

"Well, then. I hate to have missed that." He quickly glanced over the room and saw Trinon then Kur, who showed fear in his eyes as he met his gaze. "Come, Farin. Go sit in your own seat by your mother."

"Okay." Farin left his father's lap and did as he was told.

"Let's feast, shall we?" Halfar announced. He turned to his generals and said softly, "We will discuss shooting stars later, hmm?"

Coming Clean

"Did you not tell Farin that shooting stars in broad daylight should be kept secret?" Rass exclaimed, his outrage directed at Trinon.

"I did. He was probably so fascinated with it that he felt telling his father was okay." Trinon shrugged in apology. "It's not like we could keep this from Halfar forever."

"No," Rass replied. "But we could at least have a chance to put a plan in motion!"

"I thought the plan was to let them get closer to the palace before grabbing them."

Kur stood leaning against the wall deep in thought. Back in full battle gear, he was planning to participate in the second round of battle demonstrations. At the moment, he seemed frustrated with his arms clasped tight across his chest making Rass uneasy.

"Yes, that is part of the plan. If Halfar decides to squash that, we will have a bigger problem on our hands."

Trinon's expression became serious, shocking Rass at its ferociousness, as he stood to his full height with legs apart, arms folded. Always playful and never taking anything too much at heart, that is how everyone saw the young manbeast. This stance and facial expression was that of a seasoned warrior.

"Maybe not. He does trust you, right?" Trinon finally spoke after a moment.

"Right now? I wouldn't put any stake in that."

"Trust must be earned and when secrets are kept it

puts a strain on that trust!" Halfar walked through the entrance, the doors sliding shut behind him. Chardon was by his side along with Modas. "You will tell me what's going on!" He demanded.

Kur looked up from his state of reflection and made eye contact with Halfar.

"We do not know who they are. The ships are not like anything we have ever seen."

"How many?"

"Twelve. A group of four went to three different quadrants of the planet."

"Except," Rass interjected. "They are within a certain parameter of the palace. They seem to be moving in a semicircle."

"To surround the palace," Halfar concluded.

"Correct." Kur agreed.

"And your plan is to what, wait for them to show up on our doorstep?" Halfar snapped in disgust.

"In a manner of speaking. We want to get them in range for identification and then we capture." Kur explained.

"Who has the audacity to infiltrate Azrom?"

"Maybe it's the Razznians?" Trinon suggested.

"As far as we know, they have no such technology to do so." Rass said.

"If it is, then we may need to reassess their fighting ability," Chardon added.

"Not really," Kur pushed himself off the wall. "They are being sneaky, as usual. They have no more fighting skills than they did before. This would be quite bold for them though."

"I will trust you to handle this," Halfar announced. "Mark my words. If it comes down to our planet being in jeopardy, I will not stand for it."

"Agreed."

"Now, you will tell me your strategy in detail."

Gloomy sunlight cast faint shadows along the fields near Ganna's lab on New Lassa. She glanced away shaking her head in sorrow. It would take another five years for the sun to adjust itself after receiving a jumpstart years before. The efforts of both Lassian and Azromian scientists was bound to pay off. There were so many other projects on the list that she wasn't sure if all of them could be done.

On their original home world, she had created many weapons from the rich resources of Lassa. This planet did not have the same resilience and she found it more cumbersome than impossible to mold them to her liking. For now, Ganna concentrated on the issue involving the gateway and how to get a long-range weapon to work within it.

Sars held up a hand signaling his men to stop. They were at the border of the small village. It had taken them nearly eight days to travel across the barren waste land and they had to do it cloaked. That was the drawback of landing on Azrom practically blind. The quick scan of the surface was not sufficient. Their suits had enough reserve left to infiltrate the village. Afterwards it would take at least a day to recharge. He tapped the side of his suit at the collarbone and decloaked, his men doing the same.

From the view through his telescopic goggles he scanned the village. Run down fabricated shacks littered the sector with market stands set in two rows down the middle. A covered outdoor communal dining area was located near the entrance. Five hundred feet of tracks were visible on the ground, the rest disappearing into a shaft leading underground.

The robes and tunics worn by the villagers were tattered, worn out and old. Only the ones in military uniform looked halfway decent. Even those were dingy, and battle worn.

"Why is it so much different than the palace?" One of his men inquired. "Even though we are lower soldiers, our ruler still treats us with decency."

"As I said before, Halfar is not a great ruler. Not every race can have one like ours." Sars replied. "I almost feel sorry for them."

"The royals remain prosperous while their people go without. Disgusting."

"Let's continue." Sars reactivated his cloaking and his men followed suit.

They advanced into the village careful to steer away from the inhabitants. Being invisible did not mean things could pass through them. Food was cooking in various homes and small children came out of them with steaming vessels, heading towards the dining arena. Footsteps made swirls of dust as people made their way down the dirt paved streets. A strange smell lingered with the food and Sars concluded that it was decay.

Further into the village, he had his men spread out and find some discarded robes to don before their suits ran out of energy. He felt bad taking that much from the poor villagers. Azrom was not the mighty and glamorous planet the galaxy was meant to believe. Now he knew why their race did not taste very well during a fight.

Poor diet.

Some days General Kur felt he was surrounded by incompetence and this was one of them. He had sent trackers out to keep tabs on their uninvited guests. A scout from the first group arrived in the battle chamber giving a lackluster report on the four intruders heading directly towards the palace. Kur could feel a tingling in his fingers, taunting him to unsheathe his long sword and decapitate the soldier.

"Where are they?" He asked restraining his frustration.

"We believe they may have infiltrated a village," the scout answered.

"You believe?"

"We sort of lost sight of them in the middle of the desert."

The scout had a split second to rear back as Kur's long sword flashed in front of him, nicking the side of his neck. A thin line of black blood formed, and he slapped his hand over it on instinct.

Kur held the blade's end position straight out to his side, not a drop of blood on it from the speed of his strike. He returned it to its sheath and smiled. His subordinates backed away from him.

"How could you lose four aliens in the barren wastelands of our desert?"

"We can't explain it, sir."

"I can," General Rass interrupted as he entered the battle chamber.

A quick glance at the scout still holding his neck then at Kur made him raise a questioning eyebrow.

"Please, enlighten us, General."

Kur made a mocking bow.

"Tsk!" Rass walked up to the platform sitting in the center of the chamber. He tapped the edge, displaying the vidscreen. "I took the liberty of going through their footage during his less than informative report and found this." They all watched as the four aliens trekking across the desert stopped then disappeared. "They have a cloaking application within their suits."

"That does not make me happy." Kur crossed his arms.

"Nor I," Rass replied. "We do know one thing."

"And that is?"

"They are coming towards the palace."

"That's obvious! I thought you were going to shed some new insight on the situation, you being a strategist." Kur snapped with sarcasm. The others in the room took another step further away from the Generals.

"Are you mocking me?" Rass spat as his hand grabbed the hilt of his blade.

Both Generals almost got their blades out before a hand stopped them. The grip was so strong neither could move an inch and they both looked up to see who dared interfere. A smiling Trinon stood towering between them. His eyes were closed in what appeared to be exasperation which was unbecoming of the young manbeast.

"Let's play nice, okay?" Trinon spoke loudly.

He let their hands go and they pushed their swords back down. Out of the corner of his eye, Rass saw Modas standing a few feet behind the young one with a cold unflinching stare. Trinon moved away from them and let his father take over his position between the two.

"This is not the time." Modas said.

"Agreed," Kur added.

"If they are cloaked it does makes it harder to track them. Not knowing their destination means we must prepare to defend the palace."

"The palace is always protected by the royal guard."

"Against who?" Modas asked. Rass and Kur stared at each other. "These are not disgruntled villagers, they are an enemy not from this world. If they are indeed Razznian then you will have flesh eating enemies to deal with."

"Eww!" Trinon exclaimed.

Rass turned to the scout and saw the soldier was much farther away than before. He sighed heavily and said, "You're dismissed! Make sure you concentrate on reestablishing a visual. Their cloaks cannot stay up forever."

"Yes, General." The scout bowed low and quickly exited the chamber. To Modas, he asked, "How are you going to position your manbeasts around the palace?"

"There will be two at each end and three at the center entrance of the palace consisting of Trinon, Barbon and myself."

"Barbon?"

"He likes to not be seen or heard only felt in battle. He's quite introverted."

"Aren't all manbeasts?" Kur rolled his eyes as he said it.

"I'm not!" Trinon replied.

"Yes, well." And Kur left it at that.

"What about the Lassian warriors?" Rass asked.

"They are not needed for this."

Both Generals made a face and saw Trinon doing the same. There was obviously no love lost between the two factions of Lassian fighters.

"They can defend the inner wings of the palace, IF the enemy manages to get past us."

"Just to be safe," Rass began, "I would like two or three to accompany the manbeasts you assign. Better safe than sorry, as they say on Earth."

"Filthy planet." Kur literally spat on the floor in disgust.

"How vulgar. So not aesthetically pleasing," Rass sneered.

Kur's eyes narrowed. Everyone in the room knew it was not like him to do such a thing. He uncrossed his arms and strode out of the chamber without another word.

I'm angry!

It made his chest tighten as he let the thought sink in. Being infiltrated was a clear sign Azrom was losing its reputation as a mighty race.

A loud rumbling filled the air as the ground shook beneath the village. On the far end, hiding in a rundown shed, Sars and his men squeezed closer together against the wall. He covered his ears as the rumbling became a long screeching. Adjusting his goggles, he saw the cause.

Coming out of the dark hole in the ground was a large mechanical vehicle running on the tracks. It stopped shy of the where the tracks ended and made a hissing sound as if settling down. Royal guards climbed out of the sliding doors and the ones inside began to hand down crates. The villagers gathered around and took turns picking them up the crates being set on the ground.

Sars zeroed in on one of the crates and could see food rations and other supplies jumbled inside. In under an hour the delivery was over, and the guards boarded the machine. It made a loud boom and its engines whirred into action. Black mist rose from the top before the giant thing rolled backwards into the underground tunnel from which it came.

"What kind of treachery is this?" His second asked, horrified.

"It seems that is how Azrom keeps their people from starving or rebelling."

"We should be taking over this planet, not Lassa."

"You may be right. When we report back, it will be a recommendation." Sars relaxed a little and moved away from his men. "It is indeed an eye-opening revelation." He rose and motioned for them to follow. "Come. We must find some wildlife to feast on."

"We're not going to snatch an Azromian?" His third asked.

"You know what they taste like. Do you really want that for late meal?" Sars countered.

His men looked at each other as they made scrunched

up faces, then shook their heads in disgust. Knowing what they did now, it would be like mercy killings to put the villagers out of their misery. The other factor was that Azromian flesh really wasn't something to be desired. Reactivating their invisible cloaks, they headed out to the outskirts for food.

The horizon became a haze of red the color of fire as the sun set on Azrom, casting dark shadows along the landscape. Halfar stood with his legs apart and arms crossed watching the transformation in silence. A strong breeze swept his hair straight back and he closed his eyes, letting the sensation sink in. Home. Opening them, they landed on the villages off in the distance. A heaviness crept into his chest. Azrom was no stranger to wars. The last one, which he personally commanded, had left his people in devastation.

"Would you like a report on our honored guests, my Lord?"

Halfar turned his head slightly and found Rass coming up behind him. His general was in casual wear like he had been on Earth. Something about it disturbed him and he wondered where Rass was coming from.

"That would be best, General." He glanced over and saw a frown crease Rass' face.

"It has become apparent that the infiltrators are using cloaking devices."

"Is that so?" Halfar said sucking in air through his teeth. "They can creep onto the palace grounds undetected then?"

"It seems so. The manbeasts are certain they can combat that."

"Manbeasts do have optimal vision. Even so, they can't see what is not there."

"Modas is confident."

"Maybe too much." Halfar countered.

"I did request that Lassian warriors be put in standby."

"Why standby?" Halfar turned to stare at him.

"Manbeasts and Lassian warriors do not seem to get along very well."

Halfar let out a heavy sigh. This was getting tedious. The battle could not be won on a divided front. Modas was making it harder than need be.

"Make sure Talas is near the main gates." Rass cocked his head to one side in confusion. "Just to be certain."

"As you wish, my Lord."

Rass bowed low and retreated down the corridor.

"What are you thinking, manbeast?" Halfar asked himself.

Turning back to the horizon he saw that the sun had settled far down into the valley and only a hint of light could be seen, signaling the time for evening meal. He uncrossed his arms and headed the same way as Rass. As he rounded the curve, four of his royal guards step in line with him.

Jaron eyed Talas intensely, filled with concern for him as Modas relayed the plan the Azrom Generals and he had discussed. There was no flicker of emotion in the warrior's expression yet Jaron knew. Talas seethed on the inside. She knew this because she felt the same. For Modas to treat them like inferior beings was unforgivable. As his mate, it made the announcement sting deeper. Neither replied to his words and he seemed to expect none for when he finished, Modas exited the chamber.

"Mother," Trinon started.

He had stayed behind fearing the silence that filled the room.

Jaron held up a hand, halting his conversation. She kept her eyes on Talas, waiting. Even Trinon stared down at him worried. Talas began to tap a finger against his thigh, the rhythm slow and calculated. His gaze seemed far off into nothingness, yet a storm raged in it. His lower lip went inward, and he chewed on it for a while.

Jaron was about to yell at him to snap out of it when the chamber doors slid open and Rass appeared. He strode into the room and stopped dead in his tracks as he felt the atmosphere.

"What just happened here?" He demanded.

"Father brought them up to speed on the plan." Trinon replied.

"More like his own agenda," Jaron snapped. "I will not be treated like some second-rate warrior, mate or not!"

"I concur," Rass said making his way further into the room. "I have a message from Halfar for you, Talas."

Talas raised his head up and met the General's gaze. Jaron reared back from it a bit. She had never seen such a look in Talas' eyes before. Rass on the other hand was admiring it.

"Good, you're angry, as you should be. Halfar wants you at the main gates. He feels Modas is a bit too confident about going against something he can't see coming."

"That's just how Father is," Trinon tried soothing the situation in his father's defense.

"That's no excuse!" Jaron yelled.

"I'll leave you to figure out how you want to handle this." Rass left the chamber.

Trinon sat down on the floor crossing his legs and rested both arms on his knees. Jaron smiled a little. Her son had gone from being so dogmatic about everything to now taking things in stride. She couldn't put a finger on what caused such a drastic change. There was a nagging suspicion that Talas had something to do with it.

"Snap out of it!" She whacked Talas in the shoulder blade. He grabbed her wrist as she made contact and turned to stare at her in battle mode. "Talas!" She pulled away from his grasp and she saw his expression clear.

"Sorry, I wasn't paying attention."

"Obviously!" She stood up. "Modas is not in charge. This is not our planet. You need to get it together!"

"Suggestions?" Talas asked comically.

"You're the strategist!"

"So are you, love." Talas pointed at her.

"Stop calling me that," Jaron replied gritting her teeth.

Talas threw his head back and laughed loudly. Trinon clapped his hands, a wide smile spreading ear to ear. Jaron felt her face get hot.

Am I overreacting?

Sitting back down, she put on her game face and started thinking about their options.

"Since Modas does not want you anywhere near him, how about positioning yourself a safe distance?"

Trinon nodded in agreement.

"Maybe in the alcove below so you can be close, not seen?"

Talas tapped his lips and then smiled. "No." Jaron and Trinon sat up straighter. "Above."

"Above?" They replied in unison.

"I can see far into the distance and still not be in the same vicinity as Modas. The veranda two stories above the main gates would suffice."

"Sneaky," Trinon laughed.

Jaron was impressed at how fast Talas bounced back from the brink of rage. She was starting to respect him a bit more these past few years. Focusing back on the task at hand Jaron added another suggestion.

"You'll need back up. How about two warriors on opposite sides in addition to the ones Modas allowed in the area?"

"Hmm." Talas tilted his head.

"If all the infiltrators converge on the palace at once, that would put a strain on even the manbeasts, the enemy being cloaked."

"Father is not invincible, after all," Trinon interjected.

"Indeed," Talas replied. "I think we may have a plan, love." Jaron bristled.

"How come you never call me that?" Trinon pouted.

"Ah sweet Trinon," Talas laughed.

"I'm not sweet," Trinon said flatly.

Jaron swiveled towards her son at the tone in his voice. Something cold crept up inside her as both men locked on each other in a knowing stare.

"Don't frighten your mother."

"Oh," Trinon snapped out of it and began laughing. "Sorry!" He ran his fingers through his mane, smiling again.

"What was that?" She demanded.

"Nothing." Trinon, still smiling, stood up and hugged her. "I must go. Father's waiting for me to relieve him. I have to take care of Farin." With that, he left.

Jaron turned to Talas and demanded again, "What is going on?"

Talas also stood and stretched his entire body before sending a sideways glance at her.

"Nothing you need to worry about..." he stopped before saying 'love.' "He's not a child anymore, true enough. He still has a sweet heart."

"That is not what I asked, Talas!"

"Leave it be," Talas snapped. "We have more pressing worries. I will not be killed on this wretched planet."

As they both walked out of the chamber into the corridor, Jaron's own heart felt a stabbing pain. She did not like being left in the dark, especially regarding her own children.

Malfeasance

Thick fog hung over the fields just after dawn on New Lassa forcing the workers to delay their daily tasks. While they waited for it to lift, many of them went to prepare morning meal a bit early. Four male field workers opted to sit outside by the communal building unaware they were being watched, one of them in particular.

A mischievous grin formed on Mara's lips as she eyed the tallest of the men sitting against the wall, one leg outstretched with the other bent. She had been observing him for some time since the end of the Earth battle. There was something about him that she found quite charming, sexy even.

His light bronze skin and dark hair were in complete contrast to her. Plans to increase population had been brought up in early debates so she figured it would behoove her to find an ideal mate. Of course, that was a means to an end since it was also because she felt sexually frustrated. Tiny stings assaulted her eyes as her stare lingered a bit too long, straining them.

Oh, he is beautiful!

She licked her lips.

Her mother had no idea the kinds of perverse thoughts that ran around in her head. She'd probably be appalled. Mara kept most of her life private, before her death and now. She had never had a mate, per se, though she did a lot of mating on the sly. This time, she decided, she wanted true love with a permanent mate and found him.

Stepping out from behind the corner of the building,

she approached the men slowly. The three standing turned to see her and backed away a little. At least they recognized her as the daughter of a manbeast even if she wasn't one herself. Her prey did not move from his position on the ground. He did appear puzzled at her presence.

"Good morning," she purred.

"Good morning," the three replied together, their eyes nearly bulging out of their sockets. One of them clutched the front of his shirt.

"Good morning, Mara," the worker still sitting said softly without looking at her.

Mara restrained herself from squealing with glee. This was the first time he had spoken to her and his voice sent shivers all through her body, making her skin tingle. He was definitely the one for her. She leaned forward over him and waited for him to look up. When he did, she saw the color of his eyes up close. They were a beautiful gold with chocolate brown flecks in them.

"Would you accompany me for a stroll before meal this morning…" she smiled and waited for him to say his name.

"Dellus," he said.

"…Dellus?"

"Why me?" He saw his friends scoot around them and leave him alone with her.

"Because I want to know more about you, Dellus." She replied sweetly.

"I don't think a warrior of your caliber should be associating with a lowly field worker, Mara." There, he said her name again and she nearly swooned.

"Do not speak such things in my presence," she said sternly.

"It's true."

"I do not think that way!"

She stood straight. "Are you refusing me?"

He hung his head and sighed heavily then rose from the ground to stand before her. They were the exact same height, so their eyes met. Neither wavered.

"I am not refusing you. I just don't want to be mauled by any of your siblings for being near you."

"They can be very protective, yes. I will not let them harm you. Come," She extended her hand to him. "Let's go."

His gaze went to her hand and he shook his head.

"You're trying to get me killed."

Mara grabbed his hand and led them out onto the pathway nearby. He didn't resist.

On the hilltop above the communal building, Ganna sat watching the interaction between Mara and Dellus. She frowned in disgust and then laughed softly. She knew Mara thought her mating rendezvous were a well-kept secret. Ganna had seen her in action many times.

The whore has found a new toy, she scoffed to herself.

It was no secret how much she loathed manbeasts and their offspring was not off limits. She found it fascinating that the ones who were not manbeasts acted like animals in certain situations, like mating.

A thought crept into her mind and she smiled. She could try out the new weapon prototype and take that nasty half manbeast woman down a peg. Ganna assumed that she would be in the clear since Chardon nor Jaron were planet side and not scheduled for a long while. Sestis agenda was still in play, even if she was no longer be with them, with Ganna at the helm.

Working out the details in her head as she got up and walked back to her lab, Ganna eyed the two strolling hand in hand down the pathway. Stupid boy. She could never understand what men saw in the statuesque half breed. Dellus was going to learn a valuable lesson soon enough. Ganna grinned, her expression sinister.

Sars adjusted the zoom on his goggles and the gateway console came into view. Four royal guards held vigilance along with the operator. His group had managed to get close to the palace border and they now sat hidden in the dense trees surrounding the great wall. An entranceway sat below. Too obvious. That was not how they planned to enter royal territory.

Off to the left he spotted movement and focused on it. His communications team was getting into position to set up the coordinates detector. With the battalions in place outside the solar system, it would only be a matter of time before the gateway opened between Azrom and New Lassa. When that happened, they would be able to trace it and attack the planet directly before any help arrived.

"Be ready, my soldiers. The time is near for a frontal assault on Azrom's royal palace."

"Sir!" they all replied.

"This will be a glorious event."

Cloaking themselves, Sars and his group scaled up the rest of the wall and then down on the opposite side onto royal soil. Without knowing, they ran across a pressure sensor planted beneath them.

The battle chamber doors slid open and a royal guard hurried in, barely bowing properly before addressing the two Generals. His boots clapped loudly as he advanced.

"Generals!" he began out of breath. "There has been a perimeter breach on the far side of the wall! I have the coordinates!"

Rass clenched his fists. Kur unfolded his arms and placed his hands flat on the platform. Both regained their demeanor and stood straight. They made brief eye contact.

So it has begun, Rass thought.

He gestured to the soldier and the small chip with the coordinates was placed on the platform. An image of the landscape inside the wall flickered to life and small icons representing the pressure points in the ground glowed red except for one that glowed blue.

"They're headed straight for the palace main entrance." Rass spoke.

"As predicted. How did they scale the wall?" Kur wondered out loud.

"It was no easy task, that is certain," Rass replied. "Contact Modas and have him get his teams in position." He commanded the soldier.

Once the young royal guard left, Kur growled and slammed his fist down on the vidscreen platform, making the image shake. He looked up at Rass and saw the same frustrated expression on his face.

"They are bold." Rass walked around to stand by Kur's side. "If it is indeed the Razznians then we have an even more troubling issue."

"How they got here." Kur nodded as he concurred. "They have acquired a new technology. That, alone, is frightening."

"Well, let's greet them in Azrom fashion, shall we?" Rass said in a honeyed voice.

"Let there be bloodletting," Kur replied.

They exited with eight royal guards in tow.

☀

New Lassa

Six workers set the prototype weapon in place on the hilltop across from the gateway console. After nearly two hours, they were able to point the cannon in direct line of the gateway's center below. Ganna was precise in her guidance. Dismissing the workers with a wave of her hand, she admired her new toy, patting it softly. The scientists who would operate the weapon were on their way.

"Now, to get the bait."

Ganna strolled happily along the hill then down onto the pathway leading into the fields. She could see Mara off in the distance stalking her new prey yet again. Dellus was toiling away, oblivious to her hungry stares. Ganna grimaced, continuing her approach.

"Mara, dear!" She called out sweetly. The half beast turned at the sound of her name and smiled. "Here! I need you!"

When Mara was only a few feet from her, Ganna changed her ex- pression to one of seriousness. The half-breed stopped short looking concerned.

"What is it, Ganna?"

"I received word that the Razznians are heading towards Azrom. Unfortunately, I found another fleet further away. It would not be on their report." Mara's hands went to cover her mouth and her eyes went wide. "I need you to get word to Chardon and Modas quickly. Can you do that?"

"Of course! When do you need me to go?"

"It will take a bit to open the gateway to Azrom so be ready early afternoon."

"Okay."

"Thank you, dear. See you soon."

Ganna left in a state of elation. Stupid animal. She waited at the edge of the village for Mara to head home before going after Dellus. He wasn't a warrior by any means therefore unlikely to question her request. This was turning out better than she had planned.

With Mara at the gateway's entry and Ganna keeping watch, the console operator initiated the sequence to open a pathway to Azrom. As she entered the black pool swirling before her, Ganna went over to Dellus who was not far away in the adjacent fields.

"I would greatly appreciate it if you stood guard and waited for her to come back through."

"Is she not staying on Azrom for a bit?" Dellus asked confused. Ganna pursed her lips.

"No, she must deliver it and come right back. We can't have the enemy finding out where New Lassa is."

Dellus went pale.

"Then you can't let her go!"

"It's the only way to warn our comrades," Ganna said smiling, though on the inside she was close to slapping the impudent worker for talking back. "Now go! Hurry!" She watched him head towards the gate.

On Azrom, the console operator saw it light up and the gateway activate. In a panic, he tried to shut it down, his finger flying across the controls. One of the guards sped off to alert his superiors. A direct order was in place since the detection of the Razznian fleets to not open the gate for fear of New Lassa's coordinates being leaked. With horror, the operator could see that the signal was coming from New Lassa.

"Success!"

The leader of Sars' communications team exclaimed as he witnessed the gateway activation. He whirled a finger in the air and his group decoded the coordinates coming through. Complete, the information was sent to the fleet on the outer rim for the jump to New Lassa's location. In his goggles view he saw a flurry of activity around the console. He grinned, saying again, silently.

Success.

Chardon was faster than Halfar as they both ran towards the gate. His chest felt like it was about to implode, and a weakness spread into his legs. He had made it clear that no one on New Lassa was to open the gate, ever, unless he was there to supervise it.

"Shut it down!" Halfar commanded.

"I am, my Lord! It takes a moment!"

The console operator cried out. As the gateway powered down, Chardon grabbed his head and bent down to his knees. He let out a small whimper, Halfar resting a hand on his shoulder.

"It was too long," Chardon whispered. "It was traced. I know it, I feel it."

"What is going on, Chardon?" Halfar demanded. "Who on New Lassa can activate the gate?"

"Ganna," Chardon replied.

Halfway through the vortex Mara could see it start to unravel and knew the gate on the other side was shutting down. Keeping her breathing steady to avoid panic, she turned back to the entryway and into a crouched position. It would take a massive force of energy to catapult herself at top speed before it too closed. Exhaling all the air from her lungs, she launched, becoming a bullet of light.

Even at her high-speed retreat, she could feel something behind her. She had been on Azrom before and this was not familiar air. The moment her body burst through the vortex and back onto New Lassa soil, she caught a glimpse of a large ship cruising at a fast pace in the darkness of space towards the still open vortex.

Before she could stand up, a blast of heat whizzed past her, scorching the back of her robe. Out of the corner of her eye she saw it going past Dellus, blackening his right arm as he tried to dodge it. The blue beam sped down into the vortex, making contact with the approaching ship. It exploded into a burst of debris as the vortex snapped shut.

Looking up she could see Ganna on the verge of rejoice when claws took hold of her head and dragged her down the hill. Her younger sibling, Und, had the scientist in a death grip. Mara calculated what just happened and felt a twinge of hatred for the deceitful woman.

The scientists who had operated the cannon ran off in fear, not getting far since Lassian warriors blocked their path.

Mara jumped up, wincing from the pain on her back, and hurried over to Dellus. He lay in a daze trying to control his breathing. His right arm was beginning to ooze heated blood that sizzled on its way out. She leaned over him and his gaze averted from the horizon to her.

"Are you alright?" she asked.

"I'll live. You?"

Mara let out a small laugh and kissed him hungrily. He didn't seem surprised.

"I'm not going to leave you alone," Mara declared.

"I had a feeling," Dellus sighed heavily.

"Don't move." Mara commanded.

Und stopped a few feet from his sister. Ganna had been screaming 'let me go' the whole journey. He released his claws and let her drop on the ground with a thud. Medical workers came in swarms to tend to those injured from the scorching blast.

"What have you done?" Mara screamed at her.

"Did you not see? We destroyed an enemy threat before it could even get here!"

"What you have done, you egotistical creature, is give the enemy our location." Jakar came from the shadows of the setting sun and stood over her. "Do you not think they won't come back with an even larger force?"

"They can bring all they want!" Ganna spat. "We have a weapon now to defeat them. I am going to have more built!"

Jakar hit her in the head with lightning speed, knocking her out. He nodded to a medical worker to get her. Turning to address everyone in the vicinity he yelled out.

"We are now in battle mode! All warriors and technical assistants prepare posts for enemy engagement!"

The stunned looks on all their faces spoke volumes. They were not ready.

"Thank Ganna for putting us in harm's way."

Jakar walked off heading to the war counsel chamber where the head council members would be shortly.

Standing in the shadows down the corridor away from everyone else running towards the Azrom gate, Talas leaned against the wall with arms crossed. He let his head rest on it while he watched panic ensue. Something told him long ago that Ganna had her own agenda and could not be trusted. When Chardon had given her the order not to open the gate, Talas could see it in her eyes, the defiance. He was surprised how soon she had done it.

He felt a presence closing in on him from behind and caressed the hilt of his long sword with a finger. The scent of spice mixed with mild sweat let him know who it was and he moved his finger away. An arm rested on the wall above his head and he felt body heat.

"I take it, the conniving witch made her move?" Kelin whispered in his ear.

"Oh yes, and ahead of schedule, no less," Talas whispered.

"Who do you think is more angry right now?"

"Hmm. It's hard to say." Talas tilted his head back. "Are you ready on your end?"

Kelin lifted an eyebrow. "There is no sign of the enemy approaching the palace."

"Oh, they are. This was a signal to start their assault and since they are already inside the walls, I say it will be within the hour."

"Your deductions frighten me sometimes. They're always dead on." Kelin grabbed Talas by the hair and, pulling his head back further, kissed him hard. "See you after the fight."

"Be careful, my love. And stay clear of the manbeasts for now."

Turning, he watched Kelin disappear around the bend of the corridor. After a moment, he too went down to get into position. Having made himself accustomed to Azrom, he noticed the air had changed. Sometimes, being right was a curse.

With reptilian speed, Sars and his men advanced right up the center pathway of the palace's main entrance, not wavering in formation or resolve. The closer they got, the more soldiers were visible along the walls. From the looks of it, they had not detected his group's movement. Cloaked from the time they climbed the great wall, his men felt confident in infiltrating the palace right under the guards' noses. At five hundred meters from the palace doors, Sars smiled at his victory.

Modas stood guard with Trinon and Barbon at the main entrance checking the horizon for any sign of the enemy. The royal guards were ready for battle in a six-man formation ahead of his team. His agitation let him know that contact was imminent so waited until he knew the enemy's location before acting. A tense silence had spread in the area.

One level higher above Modas, overlooking the main palace entrance, was Talas and his team. He made sure the Manbeast did not notice his presence as he also waited, though not looking for the same thing. Since the enemy was undoubtedly cloaked, there would be a different precursor to their arrival. Setting one foot on the ledge of the balcony he leaned forward.

The air directly in front of the palace made a strange movement and then shimmied left to right. In that instant, Talas saw the faint glassy outline of a cloaked figure before it disappeared. Damn it! Without a moment's hesitation, Talas moved.

From above his head Modas heard a noise. Less than a hundred feet in front of him, an Azrom guard's throat was cut. He extended his claws and took a step to defend when he saw movement out of the corner of his eye from up high.

Talas catapult from the balcony with one arm and flip over into a feet first dive. Both feet struck solid air, jarring the cloaking mechanism to reveal an enemy. In the same timing, Talas swung one leg up and hit another then using the enemy's shoulder as a launching pad before hitting the ground, he sailed through the air backwards. He pivoted his body midair and landed a punch on an invisible form below him. A loud crunch was heard.

As he slid to a halt, his body turned sideways and grabbing hold of something in the air next to him threw it forward. With a thud, the now solidified enemy hit the ground, static surrounding him from the broken suit.

At a full stop, Talas stood breathing hard, coated in sweat. He wiped his mouth with the back of his forearm and looked up. The silence was deafening as everyone stood shocked in mid battle stances. Modas' face showed hostility building at the revelation his actions created.

"So," Kur purred from above. "That's where young Trinon learned that technique."

"Seize the enemy!" Rass commanded. "Get the wounded guards to medical!"

Soldiers went into a flurry around the palace entrance as Modas remained rooted in his position, fist clenched tight. His moment of glory had been stripped from him and felt his manbeasts now looked incompetent. He was waiting for the enemy to get a little closer, so his team could tear them apart and leave one intact for questioning. Seeing the guard with his throat slashed he felt a pang of guilt. He was glad to see it was not life threatening.

Modas was not happy. He had only seen two of the shimmers that were further away and assumed it was the start of the enemy's formation when in fact it was the end. How did Talas see that? Manbeasts are known for their superior vision and sensory perception and had never heard of a Lassian who could do the same. Then again, he never bothered to evaluate them as equal beings.

We made a mistake.

He turned to face his son and saw a look of dread on the young manbeast's face. After a while, Modas broke his gaze and followed the rest of the soldiers into the palace. It was a trek of despair for the defeated in his mind.

****☼****

"Did you see it?" An Azrom guard asked his squadron in a low voice. "That Lassian moved almost better than those Manbeasts."

"Our bodies are too bulk heavy to move like that," a soldier answered.

"Now wait. We do have that one village that has a species able to move that fast."

"But they are not built like us and their shells are much lighter because they have more muscle."

"Still, I think if we can learn a few tricks from them," the squad leader began.

"Have you no pride in our race?" a soldier hissed angrily.

"Pride will not win this battle," the leader snapped. "Do you not know they feel the same as we do?" A hushed silence filled the room. It was no secret how each race felt about the other. "Now, we have to because our races are forever bound. Have you all forgotten Farin?"

"Lassian and Azrom blood runs through that child's veins."

"And the Razznians have come to our planet."

"Dastardly and stupid."

"It is a bold move, no doubt." The leader stood up. "We need to convince the Lassians that we want to cooperate and let the Manbeasts feel appreciated."

"As long as they do us the same courtesy," the angry soldier spat.

"Of course." The leader added, "I am going to appeal to our Commander."

Once he was gone from the room, the other soldiers remained to nurse their drinks. Talas' moves replayed in their heads and a slight twinge of jealousy crept in.

☼

Four space podsuits were laid across the floor in the battle chamber along with the cloaking mechanisms. The pods had been retrieved after going over the terrain where they landed with keen observation. Rass stood staring at them in fascination. Such technology coming from a nasty reptilian race baffled him. His thoughts were broken by the movements in the room.

All the Lassians along with Kur, Halfar and his royal guards were also in the chamber admiring the Razznian gear. No one said a word for a long time as everyone took turns touching and inspecting them. There was no mistake in Rass' mind that the work had been contracted out by another more advanced race.

"Who, in their right mind, would sanction a negotiation of technology with Razznians?" Rass asked himself out loud.

"For it to be done so fast, means it was established long ago." Kur answered.

"So, a favor had been called," Halfar smirked.

Chardon looked ill and Rass frowned.

"What is it?" He demanded of the Lassian leader, incurring a warning look from Halfar.

"Sestis," was Chardon's reply.

Sestis II

Dreridian Council

Sestis felt empowered for setting up her first council meeting without Chardon. The gown one of her many admirers had made especially for her flowed over her body and across the floor, making her appear regal. Good impressions at these meetings were a must. This time, she only had two loyal Lassian warriors to guard her instead of the usual four. Her disgust for Manbeasts prevented her from trusting any of them with her life.

Today she would set another piece of her agenda in motion to rid Lassa of the manbeasts and Chardon as leader. Just remembering how that Azromian ruler salivated over her mate and the manbeast servant who pined for Chardon in secret nearly made her retch. Using a handwoven fan, she cooled herself down and continued to the conference room. All she had to do was sit and listen for any snippets of information to help her along so when the afternoon banquet was over, she could negotiate one on one.

The Dreridian ruler left the banquet shortly after it ended and Sestis followed him to his personal library, making sure no one saw her do so. At the entrance of the library she stopped and smoothed her hair along the sides of her face before advancing.

"Lord Pondur, abandoning your guests so soon?" Sestis cooed.

He turned his head towards her and smiled. The cragged ridges of his brow and chin made the bubbled skin seem to expand. He kept his hands behind his back and she assessed the short thick talons. She could take him if he tried to harm her.

"Lady Sestis, how crude of you to sneak around my palace unescorted."

"My apologies. How else was I to get you alone?"

"Such ambition." He faced her full on. "What do you want, Lassian?"

"We both have a wish to end the Azrom regime. They are not what this galaxy needs anymore."

"True, and they are one of the great military powers." He tilted his head. "You have something sinister in that inferior mind of yours."

"Of course," Sestis replied blushing.

"I'm intrigued. Continue."

"I have made a little agreement with their sworn enemy, the Razznians. As you know, they do not have the technology currently to combat Azrom at full force. They will have a plan soon. An audacious one."

"And how do you know that?"

"Let's just say I planted a small seed."

"And my race comes in how?"

"Well," Sestis began. Pondur held up a hand.

"Before you continue."

He went to a console in the corner of the room and pushed a button. Within seconds, a bulbous creature with craggier bubbled skin than his entered the room. "This is my chief scientist, Lord Greggor." The scientist attempted to bow, his girth in the way. "Please, continue Lady Sestis."

She stopped herself from placing a hand over her face in disgust as the scientist's tongue slipped out and licked his lips. It resembled his face; boils and crags of various size encrusted atop thick meat. Regaining her posture, she went on.

"The Razznians will need a way to infiltrate Azrom and I believe you can provide the necessary route."

"That's insanity!" Lord Pondur exclaimed.

"I did say it was audacious."

"Madness! Are you trying to get us all killed?"

"Wait," Greggor interrupted. "It is bold, yes. Also, something Azrom would never expect."

"Of course, because no one would ever actively invade the planet of the mightiest warriors in five galaxies," Lord Pondur retorted.

"Exactly," Greggor smiled and saw it dawn on his Lord's face. He turned to Sestis. "How beastly of you to come up with such a thing."

"What is it you want in return?" Lord Pondur asked, his expression serious.

"There is a small solar system in need of leadership and none has been appointed yet."

"Are you not already the leader of your own race?"

"Yes. That will end soon with the Razznian take over and Chardon on Azrom."

"You would destroy your own race?" Pondur said incredulously.

"Destroy? Oh no, I want to make it more profitable. There is a difference." Sestis again gave her winning smile. "Of course, I know this will come at a price as well. What is it you wish?"

Lord Pondur snorted and replied while looking at his head scientist.

"It is not I who will need compensation, Lady Sestis."

As he walked towards the door, Sestis grew pale and felt her stomach lurch with the banquet food preparing to exit her body by any means necessary.

"Please, use my study to negotiate." Lord Pondur left the room.

Alone with Lord Greggor, she cleared her throat and stepped to the bay windows. She could feel his eyes burning through her back as she fanned herself.

"So, Lord Greggor, what are your terms for this venture?"

"I have a fascination with off world cuisine and it would be such a delight to know the flavor of my meat before preparations."

Sestis whirled around wide eyed.

"You mean to eat me?"

"Oh, no," Lord Greggor laughed. "I want to taste you," he licked his lips again. "From the inside," he added.

"This is your stipulation?" Sestis asked softly, feeling faint. "And just how to you plan to do such a thing?"

"I have been researching your species and found that your body has multiple orifices, one in particular runs the length of your torso."

Sestis instinctively placed her hands on her backside and clasped them together.

"Is that so?"

"If you please."

Lord Greggor gestured to the table sitting beside her. He motioned with one craggy finger for her to turn around and face the window.

Her two guards and two Dreridian advisors had entered the room and Greggor made them shut the door. Sestis thought for a moment if she could get out of this and what other options may appear down the road. Seeing none, she inwardly shrugged. It was just an exploration of her insides with a hideous tongue and it would be over in moments. Well worth the greater plan of moving her agenda forward.

Climbing onto the table on her knees, she lifted her dress and gathered it around her hips. In her calculations, seducing Lord Pondur was the goal so had removed her undergarments beforehand. It now served a new purpose.

"This will seal the deal?" She asked sensing Greggor directly behind her.

Through the window she saw the reflection of him.

"Yes, indeed," he replied as she watched his tongue come out and the tip ran along the outer rim of her orifice.

Mustering all her strength to not jerk away from the slimy ragged feel of it, she asked.

"And I will have dominion of the system?"

"Absolutely."

Through the reflection in the window she watched his tongue enter her and she felt it slithering around, touching every part. He removed it and licked his lips.

"Delicious. Extraordinary."

With horror, she saw his tongue go back inside her for another taste. Sestis braced herself with one hand on the window and fought the urge to tense up. In the reflection, further back, she saw Lord Pondur smiling with pleasure.

You monster! She screamed at him internally.

The tongue slipped out.

"No tensing up, Lady Sestis. It ruins the experience."

He resumed his 'tasting' of Lassian fare.

After what seemed like eternity, Greggor was done and looking quite satisfied. Sestis climbed down off the table and let the hem of her gown fall to the floor. Shaken, she did not give them the satisfaction of showing it, as she brushed the front of her hair back down.

"Was that to your liking, Lord Greggor?"

"Indeed. You must send some fresh Lassian sometime. I think it would be such a treat."

Sestis stepped closer to him and whispered in his ear, "That could easily be arranged."

"I look forward to it," he replied softly in hers.

Lord Pondur came forward and addressed her.

"Have you and my head scientist made an agreement?"

"Yes," Sestis said sweetly.

"I will make sure to let the Razznians know of our deal." Pondur made a small wave of his arm to the door.

"Thank you, for your time, Lord Greggor," Sestis curtsied.

"No, no, thank you, Lady Sestis. It was quite enjoyable."

"Lord Pondur," Sestis addressed him as she stopped at the entrance to curtsy for him as well. He kept that horrid smile on his face the whole time and she vowed to make him pay for his actions.

The looks of horror on her guards' faces were nothing compared to the smirks of disdain on the Dreridians. She knew they would tell no one out of loyalty to their Lords. It was now clear that they felt a bargaining chip had come into play. This planet was no longer safe for her to be on alone.

"Come," she motioned to her guards. "Our transport is waiting."

Walking to the hangar, Sestis began to smile. When it was all said and done, her plan was coming into fruition. Just a few more ties to connect and her new title would be Empress.

THREE:

Keep Your Enemy Close

Dawn came with thick fog rolling over the hillside, a new phenomenon since the land had been reconfigured. The field workers made their way to continue repairing the damage done nearly a month ago by Ganna's new toy. Parts of the fields located by the gate were scorched bald and vegetation refused to grow there. A process used to regenerate the nutrients of the soil had to be administered every day for a full moon cycle.

Dellus unconsciously rubbed his right arm with the back of his left hand. The stinging pain stopped him, and he had forgotten his instructions not to irritate it. The wound itched as it healed. His three friends who always worked the fields with him came up to his side. One of them slapped him on the good shoulder and grinned.

"Looks like you got yourself a mate," he laughed. "Guess so," Dellus replied.

"I tell you what," another friend began. "If we didn't need a chief scientist with her knowledge and expertise, I would have slit that woman's throat."

"You're not the only one." Dellus started walking into the field. He didn't want to talk about Ganna or the day of the incident any more.

Halfway through his work, he heard someone beckon him and knew his plan was blown. Off in the distance he could see a council woman waving her hands to make sure he saw her. Setting his tool to the side, out of the way, he went to her. A few meters behind her stood Jakar, his massive frame giving Dellus pause even this far away.

"What can I do for you?" Dellus asked the woman.

She fidgeted for a moment and glanced at Jakar, then eyed Dellus' arm.

"If you would please go to the medical lab for treatment to repair your injury. Jakar will escort you and be on hand to observe."

"Ganna's lab?"

"Umm, correct," she answered nervously.

"Come," Jakar's voice boomed.

Dellus obeyed and followed the manbeast across the hill to Ganna's medical lab. Once there, he felt bile trying to escape and forced it back down. The scientist was sitting at her terminal working merrily along as if she had done nothing wrong. When she turned around to face them, she smiled sweetly.

"Dellus! So good of you to come. We really need to get that burn repaired. You should not have waited so long."

"I didn't want you to touch me," Dellus said with a hint of anger.

"Oh? Why, that's ridiculous. I'm a medical healer before anything else."

Dellus clenched his fists. His lips pressed tight together. The strain on his right arm forced him to loosen his fists. Jakar stepped forward and leaned over Ganna.

"Enough with the sugar coating, you disgusting monster. Fix him."

Ganna's facial expressions were struggling between indignation and sincerity. Both battles were lost and it became one of defeat. She picked up a tray prefilled with the necessary treatment for Dellus' burns and set it on the holder of the examination table.

"Please, lie down." She gestured with her hand.

"I am watching you," Jakar said as he went to stand near the entrance.

The look she gave him made it clear they would never be friends. Dellus had a thought as Ganna healed his wounds.

What have I gotten in the middle of?

Until that day, he had been just an ordinary worker who just happened to catch the eye of a female warrior. He had no intention of being a fighter in whatever battle was coming. Glancing over at Ganna he saw something nasty glinting in her eyes while she went through the motions of his treatment. Letting her touch him confirmed his initial reason for not wanting her near him. She made his skin crawl.

Azrom

There were no doors or closures for the cells located in the lower bowels of the palace and Chardon wondered how the prisoners were prevented from escaping. In truth, it unnerved her wondering about the lack of doors everywhere. Back in female form, she was exhausted from the night before. Halfar thought mating would keep her mind preoccupied from the gate incident and he was insatiable.

Her group came to a halt at a large rectangular cell with four Razznians secured against the walls. Two royal guards stood at each corner outside the cell. Halfar waved them away and he entered along with Chardon, Talas and the two generals. None of the prisoners looked up at their guests.

"Which one is the leader?" Halfar asked Rass.

"Hmm, I would say this one," Rass pointed to Sars.

"He is the most stubborn of all twelve. Has not spoken one syllable."

"Is that so?"

Halfar went towards him. Chardon stopped him.

"Wait." She nodded to Talas who nodded back and went to knelt in front of Sars.

He inspected the Razznian and then spoke to him.

"How could you have come up with such a plan? Not that your race is not ferocious. This is beyond your scope." Sars smiled in response. "Sestis' plan was contingent on Lassa's takeover before focusing on Azrom. If you are attacking Azrom then that means, you knew our race had survived." Talas stood up and looked down on Sars. "How could you know that?"

Sars cackled, making him cough, sending fecks of bloody spittle into the air.

"Earth."

Chardon's insides churned. She saw the realization spread on Talas' face as well. Razznians should have no knowledge of Earth because it was too far from their solar system.

"Spy," Chardon blurted.

"So, the Razznian Empire was spying on the movements of Azrom's ruler." Kur rubbed his lower lip with one finger. "For what purpose?"

"Broken deal," Sars smiled.

Talas held up a hand to signal his need to jump in.

"You haven't spoken in all this time and now you give cryptic responses. I'm curious."

"Whether you know or not, our plan, you cannot stop it. We now know where your race is hiding."

"It won't be that easy, Razznian!" Halfar snapped.

Chardon walked over to stand next to Talas. She waited for Sars to make eye contact and then leaned down so they were inches apart. There was no fear in the Razznian leader and made her uneasy.

"You said Earth. Were you there?" Sars nodded. "How did you leave?"

"Alternate gateway," Sars answered.

"We closed the pathway."

"Yours, not ours. Tapped into Azrom coordinates and created our own."

Rass' head snapped up in surprise along with Kur's while Chardon and Talas went pale. Halfar flexed his fingers trying not to ball them into fists. Chardon knew that the one thing they wanted to avoid was putting Earth in harm's way again which was the reason for closing the pathway.

"Why?" Chardon asked softy.

"It seemed to me, you have affinity for the humans. Maybe human race should be part of battle as well? Will you save them? Sacrifice your advantage to defeat us?"

"We need to find out the pathway they used," Chardon spun around to address Rass.

"It could be a trap to force us to open the gate to Earth," Talas warned.

Sars laughed and choked again. "No trap. We can go whenever we want."

"Well, this has turned into a three-planet battlefield," Kur announced with disdain.

"There is no way Earth has recovered from the last battle," Chardon added.

Sars swallowed hard and leaned his head back on the wall. His restraints adjusted with him as he raised a finger and pointed at Kur.

"Your enforcers made big mess."

"New plan," Talas said and walked out of the cell.

Chardon was the last one out. Before leaving, she

turned to look at Sars. There was something else he had on his mind and wasn't telling. The Razznian just stared back at her with pity.

"Let's leave here," Halfar touched her arm and guided her down the corridor.

Manbeasts gathered in an empty stone chamber awaiting their leader. Hurt feelings and resentment had festered after the Razznian attack on the palace left them standing confused and useless. Seeing their Lassian counterpart take down all four enemies in mere moments took a giant chunk out of their warrior pride. What made matters worse was that Trinon obviously had learned his new fighting technique from Talas.

Modas walked in and everyone hushed. He understood his race and how they felt these past few weeks but now was not the time to draw a line in the sand. As much strife that existed between Manbeasts and Lassian warriors, they would have to put them aside for the good of all, even Azrom.

"It's no surprise that we are now faced with a great dilemma," he started. "This war has become more complicated involving four planets, two against one with an innocent race caught in the middle. To win, we will have to disclose some of our fighting skills."

A loud din of outrage interrupted him. "But not all!" Modas bellowed over them. They stopped bickering and turned to acknowledge him. "Make no mistake, Azrom is a liability and the Lassians are still our rivals. We will only offer them a taste of what we can do."

Modas spread his legs shoulder width apart and folded his arms before continuing. He noticed the missing presence of his son, Trinon, who did not agree with his agenda.

So be it.

"We have foolishly underestimated the Lassian warriors and need to heed caution accordingly. I know some of us have mates who are warriors but, do not let that deter you from our main goal."

Movement from outside the entryway made the manbeasts turn their eyes on the cause. The Azrom commander and his elite soldiers waited to be let into the chamber. Modas motioned for his manbeasts to part and the group mingled in with them. Tension was high.

"Because we can no longer win without cooperation, we will be doing a joint training session with the Azrom forces and our Lassian race." He decided to not differentiate in the presence of the Azromians even though a slight rivalry could be seen. "Commander, please accept our teachings as we shall accept yours."

The Azrom commander nodded in agreement but Modas saw mistrust in his stare.

Good. We're on the same page.

Repairs to the battle arena were near completion and Kur was in a cheerful mood. He loved the sight of combat and bloodshed. The joint training would commence during the next moon phase which was only ten days away. Beside him, Rass strolled along quietly.

"Are you not excited, General Rass?" Kur asked loudly.

Rass stopped, causing Kur to worry as he too halted. He looked up at the sky then out into the horizon. His left hand began to shake.

"I will not be participating in such a trivial event," Rass responded.

"That's not very convincing," Kur grabbed his left hand and squeezed. "Why?"

"It's…" Rass snatched his hand from Kur's and continued walking.

Kur immediately knew the answer. Losing control was something all warriors strived to prevent in a battle and Rass had a rage within him that would lead him down that path. Neither had dealt with what happened during and after the Earth battle. Halfar refused to address it. Seeing Rass' hand shake infuriated Kur and his loathing towards Halfar intensified. There was nothing he could do to Azrom's supreme ruler, not yet.

"Then I agree. You shouldn't. The goal is to train not murder."

"I don't like feeling this way!" Rass slammed a fist against the corridor's edge and big chunks crumbled to the ground.

"Just remember, I will always be on your side."

Rass lowered his eyes and adjusted his longsword.

"This is not General like behavior."

Kur let out a loud laugh. "No, but we both know how deadly you are, so it shouldn't matter how you feel at this moment." He tugged on Rass' cloak. "Let's go check on my preparations for the events. It's quite invigorating."

"You mean aesthetically pleasing?"

"Of course! Blood shed does not need to be messy. There is a finesse to it."

Rass rolled his eyes upwards to the side in exasperation.

As they rounded the curve, they nearly ran into Trinon who was toting young Farin. Kur's eyes narrowed at the sight of the child. Instead of roaming around being pampered, the boy should be in combat training like all the other royal Azrom children. Farin confirmed his thoughts.

"Look! I have new claws!" His hands morphed into shiny black grappling claws and hit the ground.

They all watched as he tried in frustration to lift them up. His red face had beads of sweat forming and his lips pouted. With utter defeat he let them hang before retracting them back into hands sporting black lacquer talons.

"Well, at least you know how to control the morphing," Trinon assured him.

Rass and Kur looked at each other. Kur decided to recommend to Halfar that Farin be inserted in training. Claws as deadly as those should be used for the glory of Azrom.

"Very good, Farin," Rass cooed and ruffled the boy's hair.

"Trinon says he'll teach me some stuff to defend myself."

"Is that so?" Kur sneered.

Trinon smiled at him. Kur did not see the childlike prankster he usually saw in that smile. This one sent a hint of fear up his spine.

"Let's go, Farin," Trinon commanded cheerfully and bowed his head slightly as they walked past the two Generals.

"Something drastic has changed in that young man-beast, don't you think?" Kur asked his counterpart.

"Frighteningly so," Rass replied. "I think we should keep a better watch on him."

"Agreed."

Kur tapped a finger on his thigh as they walked. He contemplated on what could make the young manbeast turn one hundred and eighty degrees over a decade. Lassians were beginning to be more complex than he originally thought. He took a quick look back and was startled to see Trinon meet his gaze before refocusing on Farin.

****☼****

Pacing from one end of the chamber to the other was not helping Chardon calm his nerves while he thought of a strategy for Earth. When both forces pulled out, there was an unspoken promise that they would not return anytime soon. Reopening the pathway meant opening old wounds. He found himself chewing on his lower lip and winced when his teeth sunk in hard, drawing blood.

"Don't do that," Halfar's voice chided as he stepped in front of Chardon and licked the smeared blood from his lip. "I'm the only one allowed to hurt you like that."

"Stop," Chardon pushed him away. "I'm being serious."

"So am I," Halfar replied.

"We can't let Earth get sucked into this battle."

"Agreed. But, if our enemy thinks it can tilt the scales they will use it against us."

"There has to be a better alternative," Chardon started chewing his lip again then stopped when Halfar gave him a warning look.

"If there was a way to turn our prisoner into an ally," Halfar thought out loud, stroking his chin.

"You can't be serious?"

"Remember that saying humans had? Keep your friends close."

"And your enemies closer," Chardon finished the line.

"My race has fought the Razznians on several occasions, but nothing too serious. Trade wars mostly. For their ruler to believe we can be taken down so easily tells me how masterful Sestis' manipulations were."

Chardon felt a tinge of pity for the enemy in that moment. They did not deserve to be wiped out. On the other hand, he was not going to let his race be conquered. His pacing ceased, and he made a decision.

"I will interrogate the leader and see how far I get."

"Very well. Just remember," Halfar caressed Chardon's

cheek with a taloned finger, "he is the enemy and will do anything for his race, even if it means death."

Strong wind whipped the ends of Modas' cloak around his legs as he stood atop the spiked pillar of a tower adjacent to the palace. From high above he had a clear view of a chamber located on the opposite side where no one except royalty and their guards were allowed to venture. Larger than any other personal chamber he had seen and for good reason.

I can see it.

Four guards stood two on each side of the entrance. Two men of the royal family strode towards them and all parties gave a nod of acknowledgement. Inside the chamber, the two royals went separate ways. Multicolored sheer fabrics were draped all over the place and beneath them sat beds and large cushions. Naked bodies lay on them and some were being violated in ways that made Modas ill.

So, this is what Azromians are really like.

Modas fell backwards and descended to the lower level. As he landed kneeling with one hand on the ground for leverage, he caught a glimpse of a figure nearby. He swung around and extended a leg. His foot was caught in midair with one hand.

"That's no way to treat your own race," Talas tsked.

Modas wrenched his foot out of his hand and stood up to his full height. The Lassian warrior, never intimidated, infuriated him. He felt Talas mocked his pride as a Manbeast.

"Why are you hiding in the shadows?" Modas demanded.

"You saw it," Talas said.

"Yes." Modas stepped back from him. That Talas knew about this before he did left a bad taste in his mouth.

"What are your thoughts?"

"It's a distraction tactic." Talas replied.

"How so?"

"It's designed to keep the royals and soldiers satiated to quell rebellion."

"It's disgusting, and barbaric," Modas spat.

"Indeed," Talas replied, pushing himself off the wall. "This is how Halfar rules."

"Anyone who treats their race with such disregard is no ally of mine."

"Careful. Our races are already intertwined." Talas walked past him and headed back into the palace.

Modas stood in silence trying to get his head around what he had just seen. After a moment of deliberation, he came back to his initial conclusion. Halfar was an enemy who needed to atone for his actions. Chardon may have forgiven the ruler, but not him. This new revelation solidified his feelings towards Azrom.

The dungeon was in direct contrast compared to the rest of the palace and Chardon felt a bit disturbed by it. As a prison it should hold no comfort. Here it bordered on uncivilized. He walked the black stone corridor with care, keeping his cream-colored robe from brushing against anything. In his hand he clutched a small container with a lid by its handle. The contents swished around softly.

At the cell which held Sars and his small group, Chardon turned to stand facing into it. He saw the muscles in the prisoners' arms shaking from distress and fatigue. Nodding to the guards, the barrier was disabled, and Chardon stepped in. The first thing he did was lower the restraints to let their arms rest. Sars looked up at him warily.

"You know why I am here," Chardon began.

Sars managed a tiny smile.

"I am not going to hurt you if you cooperate. Now, why am I here?"

"Information." Sars laughed.

"Correct. It must have occurred to you that my previous mate did not have your race's welfare in mind when she brokered the deal."

"That being so, we would have strong miners and less burden on our own species."

Chardon sighed. Not only were they lacking in battle skills against Azrom, they were lazy as well? He shook his head in amazement. Looking up he saw the other reptiles eyeing the container he had carried in.

"I take it you're hungry?"

"And what is the price?" Sars asked.

Chardon smiled. "No price."

He set the container between them and stood back. With their restraints lowered, they were able to easily reach it.

The lid came flying off into the air and the bucket was passed around to each prisoner, their hands digging in to pull out a serving. Bloody entrails and miscellaneous parts slid through their fingers as they shoved it into their greedy mouths. Some fell onto the dirty cell floor. That didn't faze them. They picked them up and continued eating, the sounds wet and crunchy.

Chardon stood looking down on them, lips pursed into a thin line and his eyes wide, fascination mixed with disgust. He forced his fingers not to clench into fists as he watched them. Their diet included other species and Chardon got a glimpse of a horrible death being eaten by a Razznian. At least the creatures butchered for them in the container were killed first.

Razzna

Reptilian tails swished and collided against each other as the Razznian royal advisors bustled around the throne room in a panic after hearing the news about their fallen battle ship at the hands of the Lassians. The report came quickly and now needed to be carefully relayed to their ruler. Military heads roamed throughout the area waiting to give their best strategies for a counterattack.

The doors were opened, allowing the first set of royal guards to march in followed by Lord Kraznan and the rear guards. He saw his throne room full of agitated creatures and knew something was amiss. When they all stopped what they were doing and froze with dreaded stares aimed at him, he got a better idea of what was wrong. Seeing his high commanders also present sent alarms in his head.

"What is this?" he demanded in an almost chipper tone with a hard edge.

One of his chief advisors managed to regain movement and straightened his hunched over form. Clearing his throat, he slithered towards him, hands clutched tight together. Everyone else watched in silence, waiting for the outcome before moving themselves.

"Yes," he began. "About the strike against the Lassians."

"We were able to find them?" Lord Kraznan was impressed.

"Of course, my Lord." The advisor wrung his hands. "The coordinates were relayed straight from Azrom as Commander Sars had planned."

"Excellent!" Lord Kraznan waved his guards out of the way and stood in the middle of his throne room, scanning all the faces. "So why is there tension in my hall?"

"Well, the vortex opened to the Lassian's new planet and our fleet advanced." The advisor looked around for support and found none so continued. "The first ship was on the threshold of the vortex when it was," he paused and sought help again, "destroyed."

Lord Kraznan frowned.

Surely, I didn't hear that?

He looked around the room as well and saw stunned expressions along with fear. He would have none of that. Turning, his gaze bore in the clearly frightened advisor.

"What do you mean, destroyed? By what?"

"Some kind of long range firing weapon. It tore the ship apart in one shot." The advisor lowered his stare. "We lost many, but half of the crew was salvaged." The silence deepened.

"Why are you all shivering in your skins?" Lord Kraznan yelled in a booming voice they had not heard in decades.

His anger was palpable. Not so much at having lost soldiers in what was to be a sneak attack, but the actions of his royal council in the face of uncertainty.

"This is not our first battle and it will not be our last!"

"My apologies," the advisor bowed, shivering from the shock of his voice.

All the other members snapped out of their stupor, regaining some form of dignity. Lord Kraznan hissed, his forked tongue vibrating from the act as it slipped out of his mouth. He did not expect this kind of news after a long relaxing mud bath. Sitting down on his throne he arranged his robes to flow on the sides then waved a hand at his military advisors. The six lead commanders stepped up to form a straight line in front of him.

"I believe we have underestimated the Lassians, My Lord," his first commander stated.

"So it seems."

"This was a surprise attack but after reading the report

and analyzing the data, it is clear that the Lassians were not warned of our presence from anyone on Azrom."

"Then how did they know to shoot at the first sign of our ships?"

"I can answer that, My Lord," the third commander replied. "We were waiting for a Lassian on Azrom to contact their planet after finding out about our infiltration. That did not occur. Instead, the signal was initiated 'from' the Lassian's planet."

"In short," the first followed, "we were lured by the Lassians."

Lord Kraznan's lidless eyes opened as wide as possible and he was disturbed yet intrigued simultaneously. That the Lassians were so devious by nature never occurred to him. He leaned his large head on the hand he raised as his elbow rested on the throne.

"From the short relay the communications team sent it appears the Azromians along with the Lassian leader were just as surprised when the gate was activated," the sixth commander added.

"How curious," Lord Kraznan said lifting his head up.

"My conclusion is that there is a separate faction within the Lassian race that does not abide by Chardon's rules," his first stated.

"That weapon is a problem," the fourth interjected. Lord Kraznan tilted his head. "It can travel through a vortex and accurately pinpoint a target."

"I know of only one race with that kind of technology and a scientist callous enough to lure us in that manner." Lord Kraznan smiled with his knowledge. "That Lassian whore's companion, Ganna."

He could never forget how Sestis had sent a message to him apologizing for the slain soldier he had accompany her to a meeting in the nearest system. It was soon found out that the soldier had been sent to Lassa for Ganna to dissect as research. The sole purpose was to seek some weakness in the Razznian race. Unfulfilled rage boiled within him for a moment until he came back to the current issue at hand.

"So, we must wait for a better opportunity to strike," he concluded.

"Maybe we can lure them with the secondary plan involving Earth?" Number two asked.

The fifth commander looked over and nodded in agreement at the suggestion.

"How is the fare?" The second inquired. "If we must go into battle it would be nice to have a supply for replenishment.

"According to Sars, humans are quite tasty and full of nutrients. He put a few of the ones dying on the battlefield out of their misery."

"There is no way Chardon will let us get to Earth and start a feast," number four shook his head. "That plan is flawed."

"But," his first commander starts, "that is what we want him and Halfar to think. All we have to do is send small teams of twenty or so soldiers through the pathway we created and let them track it."

"From there, we can get to the Lassian planet directly when their reinforcements arrive," the sixth commander hissed.

Lord Kraznan liked the idea but was still a bit skeptical. Something about Earth made his stomach hurt. Good eating or not, it was a planet far behind their technology and really not worth the effort. He couldn't figure out why the Lassian leader was so compelled to protect such a species.

"What about our fleets lying in wait on the outer rim of Azrom's solar system?" Number three asked of six.

"Should we move in?"

Before sixth answered, Lord Kraznan raised a thick taloned finger to speak. He had also been thinking about this and decided on a new strategy.

"Leave them there on standby. It's too obvious that we would attack so close to this gate incident. Let's play with them a bit and see how Sars' team does wreaking havoc on Azrom."

His councilmen exchanged glances.

Finally his fifth spoke up.

"But there has been no communication since then. They all may have been captured by now."

"Of course, they have," Lord Kraznan replied sweetly. "That was also built into the plan."

Azrom

"The Razznian fleet has not moved, General," a lower officer reported.

General Kur was leaning over the digital display that mapped their solar system. He stood uncloaked in a full body tunic, his forest green hair cascading down one shoulder. A look of disdain covered his face and it intensified as he heard the update. Spreading his arms wide on the ledge, he pushed himself up straight. A swirled glint of white light flashed in his eyes and the lower soldier physically flinched from his stare.

The entry doors slid open and Talas entered the room to see the interaction between the two Azromians. He almost smiled but stopped midway and advanced towards Kur. Standing side by side, there was very little contrast. They were similar in stature, Kur the taller, with equal length of hair. Their bodies were made purely of lean muscle and both carried longswords at their hip.

Talas set one hand on the console's ledge and leaned on it a bit. "I see from your expression that you have come up with the same conclusion I have."

Kur snapped his head towards him, visibly angry. "They're toying with us," he hissed.

"Yes. Something unprecedented must have happened after the gate opened from New Lassa's side."

"Otherwise, that would have been the signal to advance." Kur finished for him.

He stepped away from the console and let it blink off while he stared aimless, deep in thought. Talas waited patiently for the General to say something. Instead, Kur turned to him and locked eyes. There was an unspoken decision flowing between them.

After what seemed like an eternity, the two averted their gaze and Talas went to the door to leave the battle chamber.

At the entrance, he turned and asked, "By the way, why the battle suit and no royal cloak and what not?"

Kur's lips curved upward. "I wouldn't want your kind to think I'm not serious during the training battles."

"Oh?" Talas raised an eyebrow. "We never thought that at all." With that, Talas left.

Strolling down the corridor leading to Chardon's quarters, Talas caught a glimpse of the Azrom sky. At midday the sun's brightness was at full force. He shaded his eyes with one hand and squinted. Before long, he arrived at the doorless entry of Chardon's temporary chamber. His eyes had to adjust to the artificial light inside.

"What brings you here unannounced?"

Chardon asked without looking up from the vanity next to the bed.

"It's midday, surely Halfar can contain his urges and wait for sunset."

Chardon finally turned a disapproving face his way, which made him laugh. Even in female form, the Lassian leader did not intimidate him much. Talas strode in and flopped down on the foot of the bed.

"What do you want Talas?" Chardon sounded irritated.

"I need you to allow a team to investigate the gate incident."

"You want me to open the gate to New Lassa?"

"Correct."

"That's very irresponsible of you. I'm disappointed."

"They already have the coordinates, Chardon. Let's not be naïve," Talas said mustering the strength to not snap at his leader. This was one of the reasons many were willing to betray Chardon in the first place.

"What did you say to me?" Chardon's anger flared along with blue light from her hands.

Talas' narrowed his eyes and he propped up on his hands. He hated when Chardon became indignant and unwilling to listen. His body flattened further into the bed ready to spring off and dodged whatever Chardon threw at him.

"The Razznians are not attacking, Chardon!" That startled her. "Do you want to know why?" He yelled at her. Chardon stared wild eyed at him. "Because something happened on New Lassa that was not part of their plans!"

Chardon's hands dimmed until the blue light disappeared. She backed away at his outburst and hit the vanity with the side of her hip, making her wince on impact. Talas repositioned his body back upwards and glared at her.

"You can't treat me like some Lassian dog! I am the leader of our race!" Chardon yelled back.

"Then act like it!"

Chardon stood there for a while in a state of confusion and indecision. Talas was annoyed waiting for his leader's reply. She eventually let out a heavy sigh.

"Fine. Take a team and go. But come back and report to me," she warned.

"Of course," Talas replied as he slid off the bed and walked to the entryway.

"I'll take Kelin and two manbeasts with me."

Chardon waved him away, traces of anger still present on her face.

He smirked and made his way down the outer corridor.

His fists clenched and unclenched while he walked. Memories of the council meeting on Lassa where Chardon decided to humiliate him in front of other planet dignitaries flooded through his mind. He shook his head to clear away the creeping rage he had felt then trying to return. In his state, he did not realize he had reached the chamber he shared with Kelin.

With two hands, Kelin grabbed hold of him, forcing him to stop walking. They were standing at the foot of the bed and looking up, Talas saw a worried look on his lover's face. Embarrassed, he leaned his head forward and rested it on Kelin's shoulder.

"What is going on?" Kelin asked stroking Talas' back.

"Our leader brings out the worst in me sometimes."

"Chardon has always been a spoiled brat," Kelin chuckled. "What more do you want from him?"

"Leadership," Talas snapped and raised his head.

"Oh," Kelin stepped back a bit. "That's a tall order, don't you think?"

"We have to go." Talas turned away from him and sat in the only chair in the room.

"Where?"

"Home."

Kelin was silent for a moment then nodded.

"Your theory."

"General Kur agrees."

"Just us?"

"We're going to take two manbeasts."

"Have you told Modas that yet?"

Kelin snorted, shaking his head.

"It's not up to him. Come, the quicker the better."

Kelin kept his distance from his mate as they headed out of the chamber and down to the housing occupied by the manbeasts. Talas felt a little bad about keeping Kelin at bay but there was no time to remedy it right now. He knew Ganna had done something idiotic, and until he had exact information, he had to hold his judgment.

At the communal housing, Talas stood at the entrance, not daring to enter a den of manbeasts with only a longsword and Kelin. The manbeasts were lounging, having drinks and conversing. It all stopped when one, then all, caught a glimpse of them. Modas glared at him as usually.

"Sorry to interrupt your festivities, but we need two manbeasts to accompany us back to New Lassa."

"And I am supposed to just say yes?" Modas snapped.

"It has been approved by Chardon. Are you disobeying our leader's orders?"

Talas put on his most winning smile knowing he had already won.

"What for?"

"Just a theory," Talas replied tilting his head to one side.

Modas nodded to the two manbeasts nearest the door and they stood up slowly with no intention of acknowledging Talas as their leader for the mission. He saw Kelin roll his eyes in contempt at the lackluster agreement.

"Don't worry, we won't be gone long."

The team of four complete, they headed to the palace's main gate console Talas could feel his muscle tighten as they got closer.

What have you done, you ignorant woman?

His fingers twitched around the hilt of his longsword.

Added Tension

Deep purple plasma warped inward then spat out towards the gate operator at the console on New Lassa, swirling counterclockwise before it went flat to form a gaping black hole. Light crept in from the middle, growing until the vortex was a white glowing orb with four dark figures taking shape. As they approached, the guardians recognized them and nodded to Jakar who stood nearby just in case there was conflict.

He had a feeling someone would come from Azrom eventually. Seeing Talas and Kelin along with two manbeasts meant Chardon was being cautious. The four stepped over the gate's threshold, onto Lassian soil, and the system was shut down.

"Jakar," Talas greeted the massive manbeast.

"We have much to discuss," Jakar replied as he turned and started walking to the commune.

A stiffness could be felt coming from the four home comers and Jakar knew what it was. There was a new kind of feeling in the air on the planet since the incident. All the people were on edge and didn't know who to trust anymore. With Talas back, he can get a gauge on what really happened.

"Why does it feel like we're about to attend a funeral?" Kelin blurted out.

The two manbeasts looked around in quick succession with confused expressions. Talas kept walking while he glanced at everything around him, seeing telltale signs of scorched soil and empty patches within the fields. Jakar watched him out of the corner of his eye and had more respect for the warrior than before.

"Not quite, but if I had my way." Jakar left it at that.

"Ganna," Kelin said and nodded to concur. He stopped in his tracks along with the manbeasts and stared up at the hill across from the gate console. "What in the name of Lassa is that?" He exclaimed.

"Ganna's new toy," Jakar replied without stopping. "Let's continue. The council is waiting."

It wasn't just the spiritual council or the scientific council. All the councils, military and political were included. Ganna was nowhere to be seen. Talas' insides felt like they were in a vice as he entered the chamber and sat down at the end beside Jakar. Kelin and the two manbeasts stood guard at the door.

"So," Talas said trying to sound cheerful. "What could possibly have been so dire that the gate was activated? Chardon is quite puzzled, as am I."

The one designated to speak was from the military council. She wiped a strand of hair from her face and licked her lips before speaking. Talas could tell it was to settle herself. She was clearly angry.

"A new weapon was commissioned by Ganna for the scientific council to create without the approval of the military council." There were hard intakes of breath from the science council. "It is that monstrosity you see on the hilltop. In order to test its power and range, she," the council woman paused. "Ganna suggested that an urgent message needed to be relayed to Chardon and requested Mara to deliver it."

"That stupid…," Kelin began.

Talas' mood sunk as he pieced it together from there without the narrative. He let the council woman finish.

"The objective was to open the gate to lure the enemy in range at the vortex entrance. Needless to say, the blast was so wide and destruction, it scorched the nearby fields along with many of the workers. It did destroy a Razznian ship on its way into the gate."

"How dare you accuse us of such treachery?" One of the science council men yelled. "We had no idea of her plans!"

"You should have asked," the military council woman spat.

"Ask what? And, even if we did, do you think she would have been honest?" He retorted, his face filling with heat.

"We did not authorize such a weapon and we surely would not have tested it here!"

"Enough!" Talas yelled.

The room went silent. His whole body shook inside, his head hung down almost in his lap. He was so angry he felt nauseous. Jakar set a hand on his thigh and forced his leg to stop moving, making Talas look up at him in surprise.

"You cannot tell my mother," he whispered.

"I can't not tell her." Talas seethed.

He found Kelin staring blankly across the room from his station at the door and regained his focus on the issue at hand. This was a travesty and the last thing he wanted to do was tell Modas or Jaron that Ganna had almost murdered their daughter. A daughter who had already died once from a planet bomb.

"Well," Talas shook his dirty blond locks out of his face. "The enemy was waiting for that. A small team of spies infiltrated Azrom and had a device ready to capture our planet's coordinates once the gate was opened from there." He saw everyone's face in the room grow pale.

"What Ganna did initiated their plans. It's great the ship was not able to get through the vortex, but now they know we have a weapon far more advanced in technology than our own. The question will be where we obtained it from."

"That is what we would like to know as well," the military council woman added.

Escorted by four manbeasts, Ganna hummed softly to herself as they guided her to the council chamber. She had no misgivings whatso- ever about the cannon's test success. From her lab she had seen the gate open and knew who- ever it was came from Azrom. Her humming slowed when she considered Jaron being one of the arrivals. That would not be good for her. Even less appealing was Chardon. Ganna pursed her lips. There was always some obstacle in the way of her and Sestis' agenda.

At the council room door, she could hear the heated tones coming from within and smiled. It was going as planned.

So Azrom was infiltrated.

Her admiration for the deceased female leader grew to new heights. One of her escorts knocked on the door twice and it swung open.

Ganna saw all the council jammed into the chamber and was taken aback. Her gaze landed on Talas and Jakar sitting at the end of the table with equal expressions of disgust directed at her. A hand yanked her arm and she looked over to see Kelin not bothering to address her as he flung her onto the vacant seat cushion near the door.

"Such dour faces, really," Ganna spoke with a small laugh.

Everyone turned to stare at her and she flinched.

Okay, they would take some warming up, she thought.

Talas seemed disappointed in her. That was disturbing. Did he expect more from her in executing the test or was he angry at her actions against the council? He was usually not that hard to gauge.

"Explain this to me, Ganna." Talas did not avert his stare. Some of the council members were about to speak when he raised one hand and silenced them.

"I thought you of all people would appreciate my tactics." She found him unmoving and continued. "During Sestis' travels to other worlds it became clear that our race was far stronger than most yet underestimated due to our lack of presence. So, she came up with a twofold scheme to rise Lassa to the top of the warrior chain."

The sound of air being sucked through teeth filled the room and Ganna smirked at their discontent. All but Jakar and Talas. Both made no motion of disdain or consent.

"Endangering Azrom and Lassa was part of the plan." Talas said.

"I wouldn't go so far as endanger," Ganna quipped. Seeing the corners of his eyes crease, she changed her demeanor. "It's no secret Sestis nor I have any love for manbeasts and if they were defeated in the invasion of Razzna, then so be it. They could spend the rest of their days slaving in the Razznian mines."

Talons emerged from the manbeasts in the room and she could see hands glowing with energy spring up around the table. Jakar made a motion with his head and the talons were retracted. Talas shook his head slowly and the council members who were ready to blast her powered down.

"That wasn't the initial plan," Ganna continued, annoyed. "We set in motion a battle that spanned three solar systems for a reason. Once the first Razznian forces came to Lassa, we would defeat them. At the same time, the others would ravage Azrom, taking them down as a superpower."

"And Chardon?" Talas asked.

"He would be done away with by being given to Halfar and Sestis would be the sole leader of Lassa. We would have a wide stretch across the galaxy and no longer looked over. We would be a new feared super power." Ganna said this with pride.

Stunned silence was the response to her explanation and for a moment she felt vindicated. No one looked at each other, or her, and it went on for quite a long time, which made Ganna realize this was not a good outcome.

"I recommend we kill her, now," the military council woman declared.

"I concur," one of the manbeasts near the door added as his talons reemerged.

Ganna went pale and whipped her head around frantically looking for a way to shield herself. Her plans were falling apart in her head.

"Stop!" Talas placed a hand on his face and exhaled loudly. "That will do no one any good." He let his hand swipe down to his neck where it rested before dropping into his lap.

"No, but it would make us all feel better," Kelin retorted.

"The technology. Where did it come from?"

Talas resumed his questioning.

"What?" Ganna answered still flustered.

"The technology!"

"Oh," Ganna stopped moving, ending in a backwards leaning position. "It was something Sestis acquired through negotiations with the Dreridian race."

She watched Talas nod twice and then rise to his feet. All eyes were on him as he slowly walked across the chamber and came to stand over her. With one hand he clasped his fingers around her neck and lifted her a good ten inches off the floor. She struggled for air, her legs swinging. In his eyes, she saw something she had never seen before in him Malice. There was no charm or aggravation, just deep searing harmful intent.

"You will come to Azrom with me," he sneered softly.

He let go, dropping her hard back onto the floor and exited the chamber. Kelin followed with a concerned expression. Ganna had never been so afraid of anything in her lifetime until now. She made up her mind then that Talas was more dangerous than any manbeasts.

Sunset brought a cool breeze carrying the earthy smells of the fields across the air. Talas stood on a craggy hilltop, arms crossed with eyes closed, breathing slowly. He needed the fresh air and time alone. Kelin was not far behind but did not disturb him and he was thankful for that. If he had spent one more moment in the same room with that woman, he would have snapped her neck.

When he accessed all the information and saw the look of pride on Ganna's face as she entered the room, he knew it was all a part of Sestis' agenda. She was quite a manipulator, he gave her that and he agreed their race was being underestimated. But, her methods were toxic, and it had caused more harm than good for the Lassians. Their home world being destroyed was one casualty too much.

Running his hands through his hair, he squatted down and looked over the valley. This was New Lassa in all its diminished glory. A planet not quite fit for their race but the scientific council was making progress. He let his arms rest on his knees and his hands dangle.

"You can come closer, my love," he shouted. "I am not so far gone as to attack you."

Kelin stepped out from behind a small hill and came to

stand next to him. He stretched his whole body upwards resulting in a few cricks and cracks. The black leather jacket rose above his hip line exposing the definition of his abdomen beneath the thin black tunic. Looking up he found Kelin staring down at him in bemusement.

"See something you like?"

"Hmm," Talas replied as he leaned backward and rested on his elbows, legs outstretched. "Maybe."

"You know I love you."

"Mmm hmm."

"I still think you should have offed her."

Talas closed his eyes, took a deep breath and exhaled through his nose. He let his head flop back and opened his eyes to watch the clouds drift in the sky. A tingling in his hands let him know how much he felt the same way.

"We need her expertise on Azrom. As capable as their scientists are, she has more information than they do."

"All because of Sestis."

"All because of Sestis," Talas repeated sadly.

"Silver lining?"

"Not so much." Talas jumped up from the ground and dusted off his leather leggings. "Let's get back to Azrom and report to our illustrious leader."

"Oh, Chardon won't like this."

"No."

"And Modas."

"I'm more worried about Jaron," Talas added. Kelin snorted. "We'll just have to try and restrain her the best we can.

"Or not," Kelin suggested.

☼

A large entourage of Lassian and Azromian soldiers awaited at the gate console for the small group's return. The anticipation of an explanation was high, and Chardon felt a huge ball of tension forming in his gut. Halfar had warned him not to expect a good outcome but there was no need for that advice. Chardon had already decided that whatever Ganna did was never in good taste.

Which is why he was surprised when the scientist showed up along with the group. She looked pale and somewhat frightened as she walked in stride between the four men. The two manbeasts behind her seemed ready to cut her down at the slightest movement. Chardon tried to undo the knots in the pit of his stomach. The news was not good.

"Talas, it's good to see your safe return."

"Thank you." Talas' tone was deadpan.

"Ganna," Chardon tilted his head. "What brings you here?"

"She will explain it all to you herself, won't you dear?"

Talas turned to her. Something about his voice sent chills through Chardon.

What happened on New Lassa?

He scanned the five faces, and none gave any indication of what it was. Even Kelin was extremely silent as if he were biting his tongue.

"Well, let's proceed to the battle chamber. Our teams await an update."

They followed the royal guards down the outer corridor and headed into the palace to their destination. Outside the chamber door, the group halted and waited for it to slide open. Halfar, his generals, the Azrom Elite and all the Lassians were present as they entered without speaking.

After everyone was settled in their respective seats, Talas turned to Ganna and his expression scared her into speaking. She relayed her explanation more slowly and with less pride than before and when she was done, waited fearfully to be reprimanded by Chardon. It was not Chardon who reacted first, but a multitude of people.

Talons and longswords were brandished simultaneously. None were as fast as Jaron who flew past everyone and landed a blow that echoed throughout the chamber, causing all to halt. Her right fist glowed electric blue as did her eyes as she stood over Ganna's motionless body. The floor below her had cracked and crumbled a few inches downward forming a crater.

Before Jaron could deliver another blow, Modas grabbed her up- raised hand and pulled her back away from Ganna. Chardon unclenched his fists and let the energy dissipate also feeling Halfar's grip holding him at bay. Talas had not moved.

"Get her to medical," Halfar ordered in an even tone.

Two soldiers gently lifted Ganna out of the crater and carried her out of the chamber.

"Talas," Chardon started but the look he gave made him stop.

"Do I condone her actions? No. But, do I agree with her assessment of our race? I do." Chardon's eyes went wide. What was Talas implying? Sestis was poison. "I'm sure Modas would agree as well."

Chardon looked over at Modas and saw affirmation in the manbeast's expression. Of all the measures taken as their leader, Chardon felt a sense of failure. Had he alone diminished his race's potential? The thought burned a hole in his mind.

"Well, it seems your former mate was a nasty piece of work," Rass broke the silence.

"She already won, didn't she?" Chardon asked softly.

"No," Halfar snapped. "Not by any means. She was

ambitious, no doubt about that," Halfar said. "I knew it the first time I met her." He turned to Chardon. "She was going to be your downfall." The memory of his first encounter of Chardon and, the now infamous, Sestis flowed in his mind.

The interstellar council was beginning right before sunset and all the delegates arrived in their full regalia. Halfar, ruler of Azrom, marched forward flanked by a large entourage of royal guards. Servants within the host palace made a wide berth. Azromians terrified them. There were rumors that his entire race always smelled of faint traces of blood and wet soil. Even the Razznians, who were reptilian in appearance with shark like teeth, did not exude such murderous intent.

As he passed the foyer, he caught a glimpse of the delegates inside and his eyes locked onto a newcomer dressed in simple robes, standing amid conversation, towering over most. His hair was a golden brown falling across his shoulders in slight waves, his skin had a muted glow. Beside him stood a female with similar features but something about her seemed false and sinister. No, his interest was in the male. All of this he observed in the blink of an eye as he continued his march towards the meeting place.

Sunset signaled for all delegates to be ushered into the conference room, filling it to capacity. The seating was arranged around a large oval table covered with delicacies from each representative's home world. Translator devices were placed at section. Shields covering the floor to ceiling windows wrapped around the room rose up to reveal the city horizon as the sun settled behind its skyline. Glow globes floating strategically along the walls flickered on, illuminating the interior.

"Welcome delegates." The host, Emperor Calabra of planet Jiez, greeted his guests. He waited for the nods of acknowledgement and looks of disdain to circle the room before continuing. "This meeting is to determine resources and needs of territories within our galaxy. I do believe we can accomplish trade negotiations to benefit us all."

He glanced around the room and saw the newcomers.

"Oh, we do have delegates from the planet Lassa. Please, introduce yourselves."

Halfar turned his gaze towards them and his eyes locked with those of the golden haired male. An unspoken vow transpired between the two in that instant.

"I am Chardon, the leader of my race, and this is my mate, Sestis." Sestis bowed her head. "Our planet is advancing in medical research and alternative agriculture. Because of this, we are also in need of resources."

"Freeloaders looking for handouts," the lord of planet Yaos snorted.

He leaned his gangly blue frame back into his seat and looked to his al- lies for agreement. A few nods occurred.

"That is not so, I assure you." Chardon obviously seemed more than a little offended judging by his facial expression. Halfar felt a twinge of pity for him.

"No need to worry, you won't be without company." Halfar interjected as he eyed the Yaosan. "Everyone at this table is out looking for something."

"Except for you, Lord Halfar! You just conquer and take what you want."

"Yes," Halfar hissed, "and yours will be next, hmm?"

"Let's keep things cordial, shall we?" Emperor Calabra raised his hands in a sign of defeat.

"Thank you, Lord Chardon. Please, be seated."

Halfar noticed how Sestis beamed at the title of Lord for her mate and could see her disturbing assumption of having the title of Lady.

She will cause his demise.

Chardon appeared not to be fond of it as he frowned when addressed. He would ask the young leader about that later.

Each delegate took turns stating their case for trade of goods and services as sunset turned into night. Arguments ensued with accusations of deceit and food was thrown out of spite by a handful of delegates. Planetary authority did not equate to civilized behavior. A long bang sounded, and everyone stopped to see where it came from. They saw Halfar's fist planted firmly on the table in front of him. A look of utter disgust on his face.

"I think we should discuss trade options individually before the night's feast." Emperor Calabra suggested nervously. Everyone, included him, reared backwards as Halfar rose from his seat. "I will go make sure preparations are underway." The emperor fled the room.

Other delegates followed suit, leaving Halfar and his royal guards alone with the Lassians. Sestis came over to properly greet herself and apparently caught whiff of his natural, after battle scent. Old blood mingled with something foul floated into her nostrils. Her eyes narrowed even as she bowed her head graciously, making a loud sniff.

"Lord Halfar, it is a pleasure to make your acquaintance."

"Your intentions are not pure." Halfar whispered in her ear as he leaned forward. "I am not to be toyed with, female." He stood back up and stared across the room at Chardon. "Tread carefully. Negotiations can be treacherous."

"Of course. I appreciate the warning."

She regained her posture and stood straight. Her sweet demeanor would not work on him. There were other delegates who may deem more willing to work with her and it made him angry.

Azrom's head of science and medical technology strolled into the medical bay and walked over to the slab that Ganna lay on. He frowned down at her as he replayed her words in his head. This woman knew nothing of Azrom yet looked down on his race. At first, he had refused to treat her then decided she was valuable to some degree. He stroked his short-trimmed beard then positioned his hand at the side of her face.

Smack!

His hand tingled from the impact and he stepped back as Ganna shot up into a sitting position, eyes wide open in terror. She blinked a few times and focused on him. He smiled showing a full set of white teeth.

"Good, you're awake," he waited for her to slide off the slab and set foot on the floor.

"Where am I?" Ganna asked scratching her head to evenly arrange her silver curls. "And who are you?" She eyed him questioningly.

"I am Lieutenant Treshur, head of the science and medical division. I believe we are," he paused to find the correct term, "like constituents. Of the same fellowship." Just thinking of her as an equal made him queasy.

"Ahh," Ganna's eyes glinted with excitement. "So, what are we going to be working on together?"

Treshur grimaced and turned away from her.

"We have some Razznian gear that is just fascinating. Come, I will show you."

He headed out of the facility making sure she followed him closely. They went down the corridor for a long stretch before stopping at one of the many sliding white doors. It opened and Ganna made a weird sound. Treshur raised his brow. Advancing further in to the chamber, he went to pull out one of the Razznian podsuits.

"Definitely Dreridian!" Ganna exclaimed as she ran a hand over the material. "They did a great job with the specifications in such a short timeline."

How she said it with childlike awe had his fingers caressing the hilt of his longsword. To decapitate the woman was so tempting.

"You know of this design?"

"Not really, but it has all their markings of expertise."

"Yes, I find it fascinating that they had dealings with the Razznians. Your Sestis was a venomous woman." He watched her face scrunch in offense at his words. "Our goal is to duplicate the specifications."

"Oh?" Ganna said as she glanced at him out of the corner of her eye. "That would prove time consuming. We can, however, create something like it in less time."

Treshur let his lips curve into a huge smile.

"Exactly what I was thinking."

She had performed just as he had imagined. His task was to get out of her the name of the race responsible for the podsuits and it turned out to be easier than he thought. How proudly the female scientist boasted of her disgusting agenda and experimental findings.

Dreridians, hmm?

Those cunning aristocrats were indeed highly intelligent.

"I will leave you to it, then." Treshur waved a hand as he went to the door.

"You're letting me do the discovery myself?"

"Oh, there will be others soon to help."

He left the chamber and went to report to the generals. Rass, he knew, would especially be pleased.

General Rass slammed his fists on the vid console and tried to control his breathing. Halfar stood only a few feet away from him, tapping a talon against his bottom lip. A frown creased both of their brows. Kur found it amusing.

"Why so distraught?" Kur asked. "We all know how devious the Dreridians are, let alone a foul indulgent species."

"Partnering with Razzna? That's not just an all-time low, but a slap in the face to the warrior clans in the galaxy!" Rass yelled back in response.

Halfar turned away and sat down in the command chair at the end of the console. Dark thoughts swirled in that tyrant brain of his. Kur cocked his head to one side and waited for his Lord's brilliant idea, or insane theory.

"They are playing a dangerous game." Halfar finally spoke. "Sestis is no longer a factor so their main goal from the beginning was to take down Azrom from within."

Not so insane.

Kur was actually impressed that Halfar came up with it before Rass who also looked over in surprise. Which didn't prepare him for what came next.

"Let the Razznians escape."

Kur blinked a few times to alleviate the shock coursing through his system. Even Rass shot up straight incredulous at their ruler's suggestion. And within seconds Rass had a new kind of expression on his face, something sinister. He liked it, feeling a tightness in his groin.

"Ahh," Rass exclaimed. "Yes, they would immediately rendezvous with their fleet sitting on standby outside our solar system."

"Tsk, tsk," Kur wagged a finger.

"They would be aware of us following them."

"Yes, but not before retrieving the podsuits hidden somewhere in the desert." Rass smiled.

"What are you getting at?" Kur was confused.

"I have a way of taking over the main fleet's weapons system."

"And all you need is a podsuit we have not tampered with yet," Halfar added.

"Why would you want to…?"

Kur stopped and decided to ask no further. It seemed they were on a wavelength he had no knowledge of.

"I believe Chardon would be our best bet," Halfar suggested.

Kur rolled his eyes in exasperation. One day, Chardon was never going to forgive Halfar for the horrible situations he planted him in. Done with the whole insanity of the plan, he walked out of the battle chamber. He needed to prepare his enforcers for a Razznian escape.

Since the initial set up had been disrupted, Sars waited to move forward with plan B. His group was supposed to be the only one captured while the others planted seeds of destruction around Azrom, especially in the palace. Now he had to get at least one of the other teams out of the holding cell. As the leader, he would stay inside. All he needed was a window of opportunity. Hearing the familiar footsteps of his regular visitor, he grinned.

Chardon came into the holding cell and scrutinized the Razznians. He held another bucket in his hand and for a moment, Sars craved it. He eyed his comrades and they got the signal to stay. Caving in to hunger was not the first step in escaping.

"I see we are going into a defiant mode," Chardon

stated, and it made Sars think the Lassian was reading his mind.

"Just making a stance against our captors."

"I am not your captor," Chardon replied. "You were stupid enough to infiltrate Azrom. They are your captors."

"Do you even know about this planet? Your mate?" Sars shook his head sadly at Chardon. "How blind you are."

"My vision is clear, I assure you."

"You know nothing!" Sars snapped.

Chardon dropped the bucket onto the floor and his hands glowed red. Sars backed further against the wall.

"This planet has secrets you have not seen," Sars said, then smirked.

At that Chardon hesitated and Sars stared at him as the Lassian glanced upwards in contemplation. From his view on the floor he realized with awe that the guards had not activated the shield, again, because Chardon was there. Sars cursed himself inwardly as he ran each visit in his head and saw the same scenario. He could have executed his plan B long ago.

No. This was good.

Because Chardon fed them, his men had more strength to fight. Sars made guttural clicking sounds that communicated his idea. It also broke Chardon's reverie and he looked down on them knowing instantly what was about to happen.

His hands glowed a bright orange and the team of Razznians on the left of him snapped the restraints. They tackled forward, sending Chardon flying into the wall opposite the cell. He was back up faster than they thought. Sars watched in dismay as a hole was blasted into one of his men and a chunk of another's abdomen disappeared.

Blood sizzled, dripping hot on the floor. Two more Razznians got loose advancing forward, grabbing the bucket to toss at Sars.

Outnumbered, Chardon moved further down the corridor even as Azromian soldiers bustled in to assist. Sars remained still as he saw six of his men get past the guards and Chardon. He could hear screaming in the distance and the familiar sound of blood gurgling out of a wound. Nodding in satisfaction, he opened the bucket and motioned for the remaining three to join him for dinner.

This is not how it was supposed to happen!

Kur walked briskly to the east side of the palace to see what he could salvage of Rass and Halfar's insane plan. There were casualties from Razznians taking the liberty to chew on his soldiers in defense. He drew his longsword hearing cries of battle and agony ahead of him.

Rounding the curve of the outer corridor he came face to face with a Razznian baring razor-sharp teeth coated with Azromian blood. Kur swung and was surprised that he missed when the Razznian flipped backwards to avoid the cut. He increased his speed and the Razznian did the same to keep up with him. Tiny lines of blood appeared on both their bodies as they switched off getting some hits in but nothing fatal.

Kur lunged at him in frustration and watched the Razznian jump off the ledge and land on all fours down on the planet floor. Looking over, he could see four of his soldiers go down, their necks spewing blood from the gaping holes left by the Razznians' bites. A cruiser from the hangar was hijacked and off the enemy went speeding towards the desert on the other side wall. He gripped the ledge hard.

Turning back the way he came, Kur headed for the palace command center where he knew Rass and Halfar would be waiting.

The escaped Razznians made haste to the first rendezvous point where four of the podsuits had been hidden. Once donned, they split up into pairs while the remaining two took the cruiser and headed to their hiding place. Time was of the essence. They could see Azromian forces cutting across the desert in a storm of dry dirt whirling towards them like a tidal wave. With only moments to spare, the two made it to their suits and activated the cloaking.

Running at a fast pace, in teams of two, each pair found the drop sites and dug up the containers that were previously buried. It took two to lift and open them. Inside were weapon launchers, bomb cartridges included. The collapsible targeting tripods were erected to stabilize the launchers when firing.

Team one now consisted of the last two communications officers and their job was to give the signal after contacting the main fleet. They set the array and waited for a reply from command.

"This is madness!" Kur yelled.

He had stormed into the command center and found Halfar and Rass dumbstruck by the turn of events. A large unit was dispatched after the escapees but lost them just as they were closing in. From the reports flooding in it was apparent that the group went separate ways.

"Those damn cloaking devices," Rass exclaimed.

"I don't care about that," Kur said drawing out every syllable. "I have dead soldiers!"

Halfar whirled on him and stood face to face.

"I know!" he seethed.

A royal guard came into the room and bowed low. His face was grim.

"What is it?" Halfar demanded, yelling.

"Incoming, my Lord."

"What?" Halfar reared back in surprise. Rass grabbed the guard by the front of his tunic.

"Heat signatures from three directions heading towards the palace." Rass pushed the guard away and fled from the room, grabbing a commlink amplifier. He connected it to the side of his cheek and gave an order.

"All defense forces take position at the impact points and form a barrier! The palace must be protected at all costs!"

Kur followed him out but went the opposite way. Further down the corridor he ran into the Lassian energy users, led by Jaron. He didn't need to ask her anything, she just nodded.

"I will have my team position themselves between the gaps in the impact points and see if we can deflect some of the damage."

"I owe you my gratitude," Kur bowed low to her.

"Stop that! This is no time for that drivel." Jaron left with her entourage in tow.

Looking up at the horizon he sucked in air as he witnessed the large beams of heat carrying destruction streak across it from all three sides towards the palace. There was no time for training sessions now. It had begun. Knowing what was coming next, he headed for the hangar. A Razznian battle fleet was on its way and he was going to make sure to greet them properly.

Three groups of eight soldiers stood behind barriers at each corner of the palace while they watched the beams come full force at them. As they struck, the soldiers lost their footing causing a breach in the barriers integrity.

The blast blinded them and sent their bodies backwards. Thin fissures began to form along the barrier's edges. Not anticipating how wide the beam was, they watched in horror as it overtook the shielded areas and slammed into the exposed parts of the palace.

Jaron and her team were able to deflect some of the blast but where the stray beams landed was a problem. The wall separating the palace from the rest of the planet was decimated in large spots along its perimeter. Even the hangar was hit, most of the cruisers destroyed.

Kur did not flinch from the blasts of cruisers exploding around him as he made his way to the elevator on the far end of the hangar. His stride was slow and purposeful. At the elevator he waited for it to open then stepped in. It slid shut and descended into the bowels of Azrom. Reaching its destination, the doors slid open.

Azrom's mighty Armada was spread farther than the eye could see at ten thousand ships strong. Soldiers were already preparing for battle making way to their assigned ships. From the other side of the cavernous underground hangar, the other elevator opened and Rass came charging out. He stopped for a moment to stare at Kur then resumed his advance.

The two generals met in the middle at the front of the Armada and stood side by side watching one hundred of the ships power up.

"This may be overkill, you know," Rass quipped.

"Nonsense," Kur replied. "A show of force is necessary."

"Oh?" Rass' brow curved upward. "What about aesthetics?"

"That can wait for another time."

"I wonder," Rass continued. "How surprised would they be when our ships launch from underground?"

"They should have known better when they didn't see

a single Armada ship anywhere on the planet surface."

Kur snorted afterwards.

"I guess the battle is at hand."

Halfar's voice boomed through the cavern.

"Victorious!"

"Til death!" Every soldier including the generals roared back.

Rass and Kur went to their command ships, their thirst for battle increasing.

Anger fueled Chardon's running speed out of the lower region of the palace and into the blinding aftermath of a Razznian weapon's impact. The wall beside him crumbled, causing the floor beneath to sway. Dismissing the wreckage, he kept on until he came in contact with a wounded royal guard.

"Where is Halfar?" Chardon demanded.

"Command Center," the royal guard replied breathlessly as he slid down to the ground.

Chardon looked around at his surroundings and catching his bearings went straight to where Halfar was. He made it, without being scathed further, to find Halfar in a foul mood and his soldiers in a panic.

"Your incompetent guards left me unprotected with the shield down!"

Halfar didn't turn to face him but answered, "I know."

"You know?" Chardon shrieked, incredulous.

"That was part of the plan, but as you can see," Halfar waved an out- stretched arm across the console in front of him. "I miscalculated and didn't expect this."

He finally looked at Chardon and noticed the blood. By the scent he knew some of it was Chardon's though mostly Razznian.

"Are you hurt?"

A ball of golden light expanded around Chardon and electricity shot out haphazardly, zapping equipment and soldiers. The smell of charred flesh filled the air and Chardon yelled in a fit of rage, the heat intensifying. Halfar's eyes went wide with fear.

The ball of light pulsed inward and before it could expand back out, Chardon went limp, crumbling to the floor. Standing behind him was Modas, calm as ever.

"This is your doing?" Modas asked, glancing back at the doorway.

Halfar held one arm up with the other laid across his chest. He stared at the manbeast trying to gauge what the next move would be.

"I made a mistake."

"War has begun then."

"Correct."

Modas lifted Chardon off the floor and threw him over his shoulder like a sack. He left the room as silently as he came in, stopping in the entrance for a second before turning left.

Research equipment shook violently then slid across the lab slamming into scientists with nowhere to go except against the walls. Ganna crouched down low onto the floor and braced herself by holding tight to an examination table. Hairline fractures snaked up the walls and she felt a sense of panic. Her plans did not entail dying on Azrom. From the deafening booms she knew the Razznians had attacked which meant they were on their way to New Lassa.

Ganna gripped harder, her hands balled into fists. It finally dawned on her that luring the enemy was not the best choice.

Would they have found New Lassa eventually?

Of course, but her actions led them right to it.

What have I done?

The doors slid open and three Lassian manbeasts bore down on her, wrenching her from the table. More Azrom soldiers entered behind them to rescue their own people. Swiftly, everyone was carried out of the crumbling research lab. She didn't like the way the manbeasts were handling her so roughly but dared not complain.

"What's happening? Where are we going?" She cried.

"Be silent, monster!" The manbeast to her right barked out at her.

"Let go of me! I can flee on my own two feet!" She tried to get out of their grip but they held on even tighter to the point of hurting her.

After maneuvering through dangerous routes filled with falling walls and debris, they reached a platform that was still intact: the gateway. Chardon lay in a heap on the ground while Jaron and Modas checked to make sure all parties were present.

"Open the gate!" Jaron demanded.

The guardian made haste with the coordinates on the console and the pathway to New Lassa burst open.

"You," she pointed to a Lassian warrior and Azromian royal guard. "Take Farin and escort him through. Modas, grab Chardon." Jaron turned to the portal. "Let's go!"

"Why are we leaving?" Ganna asked.

"Because the enemy is going to jam our coordinates in the next hour and we will not be able to help our people defend New Lassa," Jaron snapped. "If you hadn't interfered, we would have at least two more years to prepare. So," Jaron glanced back at her. "We thank you, Ganna." The sarcasm dripped with venom.

Before Ganna could respond, she was pushed forward through the gaping vortex.

FOUR:

Let the Battle Begin

Soon after returning to New Lassa all warriors were given instructions on where to be positioned and what tasks to complete. As the leader of his race, Chardon took charge of evacuating the civilians while Jaron held various meetings with the military council. Eyeing the giant cannon resting on the hilltop opposite the gateway console he wasn't sure whether to embrace or hate it.

Securing the last latch on the underground bunker, Chardon headed back up to the surface and breathed a sigh of relief that most of his people would now be safe. Atop the hill was a group of scientists led by Ganna fiddling with the cannon, preparing it for action. His left eye twitched and he tasted bile at the back of his throat. Her existence now made him physically ill. He went up to observe.

"Chardon," the four scientists greeted him in unison, bowing their heads slightly.

"Is it almost ready?"

Ganna looked over at him with a forced smile.

"Shortly. I'm not sure it will take them by surprise this time, though."

"No," Chardon narrowed his eyes and looked away from her. "But we can at least shoot down a few ships as they come through."

"Chardon," Ganna started.

He turned and walked off.

"Don't," was all he could muster.

There was silence as everyone waited for the gateway to activate and spew out enemy ships. Hours went by but they all stayed vigilant, watching the sky above the console. Right before dawn, it happened.

The sky ripped open on the horizon and a vortex as wide as a mountain appeared. Slow and steady, a large fleet of Razznian ships invaded New Lassa. When the cannon took out two at once on the formation's edge, fighters spilled out of the larger ships like a swarm of insects and spread out across the terrain.

Jaron created a giant ball of energy and flung it into the swarm in front of her. Some exploded in midair while others crashed down on the planet floor and their occupants sprung out. Manbeasts were ready in a flash to greet them with hand to hand combat. More Razznians came raining down from the ships as they passed over towns, flooding the area with foot soldiers to wipe out anyone who was still standing from the bombardments.

Teeth and talons clashed, creating portraits of blood splatter. Und led a small group of manbeasts to a deserted town now crawling with blood thirsty carnivores and immediately found himself deep in a bloody haze. He tore into the thick reptilian skin of an enemy and got a taste of Razznian blood on his lips. Spitting it out, Und grew angry.

He didn't even feel the teeth bite into his shoulder, only that an enemy was on him. Reaching over he punched his talons into the Razznian's head, yanking him off and into the waiting claws of another manbeast.

Blood dripped from his wound, yet he didn't stop. There were so many enemy soldiers. A burning heat piercing his shoulder followed by sizzling made him growl out in pain, his body arched backward. The pain subsided, and he turned to find one of his litter sisters backing him up along with a few other energy users.

"Get it together, brother. We have to wipe them off the face of our planet."

Through stinging eyes caused by sweat, he took a deep breath and nodded.

"Let's have some fun then." She smiled, taking out an enemy with one ball of yellow energy without looking away from him.

"Impressive."

"Oh, you haven't seen anything yet," she winked. "Shall we?"

Three energy users and five manbeasts formed a circle and launched themselves into the fray.

From the dark side of Azrom's moon, the Razznian fleet appeared and was met by a defense line of one hundred ships from the Azrom Armada forming a curve four rows deep around the planet. The enemy fleet maneuvered into position in front of them and both sides sat in stillness among the stars.

They simultaneously opened fire, creating a bright criss cross light display. Ten of the Razznian ships broke formation and advanced towards the lower barricade of Armada ships. After four of the Azrom vessels were shot down, careening to the planet surface, the remaining seven enemy ships gave pursuit.

General Kur watched the interaction and realized the enemy's strategy too late. He stepped away from his command post and began to shout out orders.

"Tighten the formation and don't let another enemy ship past our defenses! I want fighters deployed now!" He walked to the doorway and paused. "I'm going out!"

There was a heavy silence. No one dared speak up.

Good.

Kur took another step forward and the sliding doors opened. It had been a long time since he battled in a fighter, so he knew what his crew was thinking. He was more of a hand to hand combat type of soldier. Right now, the situation called for his second expertise despite rusty he may be. At the ships hangar, he found a technician finishing up the diagnostics run on his fighter and waved him off.

He threw off his cloak, tossed his longsword in the side compartment and donned the battle flight suit handed to him. Pulling it on, he leaped into the cockpit and let the system mold around him, securing his body. A vidscreen helmet settled over his head and it activated so he could see through the lens of the fighter.

"There will be six fighters accompanying you, sir. Is that enough?" The technician inquired.

"That's fine."

The fighter closed, and the internal systems engaged. He opened an outside channel. "If this ship falls, I will kill every last one of you. Ready for launch!"

Kur's fighter shot out of the hangar with six others following in a 'V' configuration. He could see eight other teams of fighters converging on the enemy and twisting sideways veered towards the main ship. His men kept in line directly behind him.

"What in all of Azrom are you doing?" Rass' voice spilled out into the cockpit.

"Fighting," Kur replied nonchalant. "No need to yell."

"When was the last time you actually fought in that thing?"

"It doesn't matter," Kur replied as he opened fire, sending a rain of explosive charges at a small group of Razznian fighters. They lit up in a ball of light.

"I'm enjoying myself immensely."

"Get back to your ship!"

Kur didn't need to hear anything more. He could tell what Rass really wanted to say. Feeling just a tad guilty, Kur sighed and replied.

"You're not going to lose me."

Silence. Then.

"Good hunting. See you back planet side."

Kur's unit kept in tight formation as they curved around towards the aft of the Razznian's main ship. They were able to glide low enough to avoid the onslaught of attacks by being out of range. Kur searched for a weak spot in the underbelly and finding it, ordered his unit to fire. As they swooped upwards out to the other side for safe distance, the ship shook, and an explosion spread throughout its length.

Out of the corner of his vision, Kur saw a ship in the middle charge forward, its main weapon gathering energy. It rammed into the damaged main ship, pushing it to the side out of the way then corrected its own position.

"No, no, no!" Kur cursed.

Too late, he realized his unit was heading straight into its line of fire with no time to adjust their coordinates or speed. He watched the ship's main weapon fire and his fighter was clipped on the side, the two fighters on his two and six obliterated. He called up every maneuver from memory to keep his fighter from exploding as it fell through Azrom's stratosphere.

Getting closer to the surface he could see ground combat in full swing and he was going to crash right in the middle of it. Off in the distance the blast from the Razznian ship hit the palace directly in the middle at its top. Energy users were bent down almost to their knees, arms upraised as they blocked the attack. It only lessened the damage. The beam was wider than their coverage and the area outside the blast caved in. Knowing there was nothing to be done, he braced for impact. The fighter hit hard forcing it to slide only so far before making a dead stop. Disengaging the system and opening the hatch, he grabbed his longsword and jumped down onto the planet surface.

Within seconds, two Razznians came at him, baring sharp teeth and thick claws. Kur smiled. This was more his forte. No hesitation, he ran to meet them halfway. His sword sliced through the air, missing the one closest to him. He morphed the other arm into a claw and snapped the Razznian in half midair. The other enemy charged him in a fit of rage, making Kur laugh.

"Come! Join your comrade in arms in death!"

He brought his word down to cut the Razznian in half and it reversed its advance in barely enough time to only get a deep cut across its chest. At the same time, Kur felt multiple presence behind him and turned to face them, quickly dodging from a strike mere inches from him. More Razznians were behind him. He was surrounded.

A blade went through the one before him and the enemy was yanked backwards as the one next to him peeled apart at an angle from the left shoulder to the right hip. Standing on the opposite side was Talas, gleaming with joy, flecks of blood splatter in his dirty blond hair.

"That was quite a landing, General," Talas laughed as they assumed a defense stance back to back.

"I like to make a grand entrance."

"A little rough up there?"

"Nothing we cannot handle."

"Good to know." Talas raised his longsword. "Shall we?"

"Let there be blood."

"Indeed."

Walls crumbled in large chunks exposing the innards of the palace. Halfar pushed himself up off the scorched, debris filled floor of the command center and stood. For a moment he was baffled by what had happened then rage took over. Azrom had not been attacked in such fashion in four, maybe, five hundred years. An attack that prompted the start of a long war with an enemy far more formidable than Razznians.

He surveyed his surroundings and headed out into the open air. All the soldiers in the command center were down, half of them dead. The survivors would have to hold on and wait until after the battle had died down or was over. Halfar found the stairwell leading down into the lower parts of the palace which were still intact and made his way to the bunker below.

At the entrance, two royal guards bowed deep and opened the doors. The brightly lit room spanned for what seemed like a mile with consoles lit up and their operators in constant motion. They all stopped for a brief second to bow low at their ruler then continued their work.

"I want the cannons online." He spoke in normal tone.

"Yes, my Lord!" the first row of operators replied.

"Target?" The head operator asked.

"The gate."

There was a pause in the room. "My Lord?"

"Open the gate to Razzna's system."

"Calculating the coordinates now."

"My Lord!" The second operator cried out. "The gate has been disabled. It's locked for some reason!"

Halfar smiled, knwing that would happen. Walking over to the commlink, he selected a sequence code.

With audio only, he delivered his order.

"Rass, I need you to open the alternate gateway to the Razznian system."

"Of course, my Lord. Sending the location to the operations center."

"Good."

"Are you angry?" Halfar didn't reply. "Excellent. They did not anticipate this."

Halfar sat in the command seat overseeing the bunker. He watched from the vidscreen as two of the cannons ascended to the surface, the hangar doors sliding open to accommodate them. The giant orbs rotated towards the alternate gateway forming in the horizon. It expanded, the gaping hole of swirling black and purple clearing to reveal the Razznian solar system beyond.

"Ready cannons for firing."

The operators went into a flurry, their fingers flying across consoles. The giant orbs began to glow bright blue and the lenses inside adjusted once more for accuracy. A gauge on the right side of the vidscreen showed the increase levels of the cannons' energy. When it hit full power, Halfar sat back in his seat.

"Fire." He didn't need to yell.

The terrain shook as the cannons recoil vibrated down into the surface. Many of the combatants on the ground were thrown off their footing, away from their opponents. Some of the Razznians looked up and saw the vortex in the sky, the blast of the cannons heading straight for their home world in the distance.

Kur took a gander at Talas and the Lassian's lips pursed out as he nodded.

"Not bad. This will tilt the advantage in our favor." Talas nodded towards the enemy standing stunned for a few seconds before going into a frenzy. "They definitely want to kill us all now."

"So be it," Kur spat. "Azrom will be victorious!"

"You do know, we are fighting on New Lassa as well?"

"I have no concerns over that. Your race proved to be a hard one to kill off."

Four long talons went through the side of a Razznian advancing towards them and the body was tossed away. Modas strode up to them, calm and collected, while slashing down Razznians. Opposite him, a group of enemy combatants went flying outward, blood misting above Trinon in the center.

"Good of you to join us, manbeast," Kur said with an edge of malice.

He had not forgiven the warrior for his near untimely demise back on Earth.

"The enemy in the East has been dealt with," was all Modas reported. "Well, there are three other quadrants to clean up then," Talas quipped. "But, first," he nodded at the nearly one hundred Razznians still on the ground surrounding them.

"Let's make this quick."

Modas tilted his head forward in agreement. Kur wiped the blood from his longsword on the leg of his battle suit. The Razznians looked hungry.

Chardon couldn't believe how many ships had come through the gateway. Though it had only been seven, he expected one or two. He didn't understand why the Razznians would send more than that for a nearly wiped out race on a barely sustainable planet. His robes were covered in blood, very little of it his own. The ground was partly scorched, yet again, and the cannon had been damaged from a direct hit by the ships weapons.

A Razznian leapt into the air and came at him. Tired yet no less focused, Chardon shot an orb of red light at him. Burned to cinders, the enemy crumbled, the wind carrying the ash remains away. He was keeping his full power at bay because it would devastate the planet more than it had already suffered.

"We can't go on much longer," Jaron spoke to him out of breath. Her hair was matted and sweaty.

"I know, but we have to protect this planet to the very end. It is the only home we have, and we just got it."

"As powerful and capable as we are, this is beyond our expertise." Jaron formed a barrier around them. "We are a ground combat warrior race. We don't have a battle fleet of ships. You have to destroy them all at once."

"I will not harm this planet!" Chardon yelled.

Jaron whirled on him and got so close they shared breath.

"There will not be a planet if you don't!"

"I can't wield it knowing how many will get caught up in it!"

Razznians converged on the barrier desperate to get at their prey.

"The planet can be fixed! And so can our bodies! What the hell is wrong with you? Stop being spineless and be our leader!"

Chardon's face darkened, his hand went to strike her. She blocked his blow and grabbed it. Her expression was one of rage and disappointment. Outside the barrier Jakar was killing off the last of the enemy who had been clamoring to get through.

"Now I see," Jaron continued. "This is what made Sestis and Talas so frustrated."

Chardon wrenched his hand out of her grip in anger. He was sick of hearing what in his mind was not true. He understood there were times when he wavered and the outcome not ideal. Looking up at the ships spewing out more fighters, he decided.

"Release the barrier." Jaron did and Jakar stood next to her. "Try to get as many to an underground shelter and make sure Ganna is with them." They both frowned. "You think I want her to live? I want to rip her apart. But for now, she is the chief medical officer."

"Will do," Jaron replied. To her son, she said, "Let's go." She stopped and turned. "Oh, the group ahead will make sure no enemy gets near you."

"But, that means…" Chardon blanched.

"Yes, some of them may be destroyed completely. They know that, Chardon." Jaron snapped.

He watched them leave and Lassian warriors took their place to keep the Razznians at bay. In the sky above, the remaining ships kept advancing further into the planet, firing rounds down on the surface. Shaking his hands to loosen them up, he took a deep breath then exhaled slowly. Tears stung his eyes. To save his race, he had to sacrifice many.

A large knot tightened in his stomach, forcing him onto the ground. He wailed in agony holding his midsection tight as his head fell back. Leaning forward, his hands planted on the ground, he stared at the enemy. His body glowed in an array of colors, swirling, building up around him and expanding out. As it spread miles wide in diameter, the air hissing in complaint, it pulsed once, retracting back to him in a nanosecond.

The blast shimmered like multicolored jewels engulfing the entire planet's surface and sky. Everything in its wake was slowly eaten away, disintegrating into nothingness. Screams from Lassian and enemy were short lived. The only safe place was the eye of the storm that was Chardon, hunched over full of despair as he unleashed his power.

Inside, there was silence.

Surrounded by chaos, Sars sat patiently as he felt the palace walls around him tremble then crumble. His men kept guard in case anyone came back down into the dungeon. Hours went by and finally, he heard the click clat signal echo through. All six hurried into the now broken cell and helped their comrades.

"Bad news to report, sir," The first said.

Sars brushed his hands on the legs of his tunic and frowned. "Tell me."

"A vortex was opened to our solar system and Azrom sent two cannon blasts through it."

"Our planet will be destroyed?" Sars' lieutenant cried.

"Not destroyed, but," the Razznian lowered his head. "It will be bad."

"So we can't go back home."

"We locked the gateway."

"Then we must unlock it." Sars commanded.

"And go where?"

Sars smiled or what appeared to be the closest thing to one. "Earth." His men gasped in disgust. "It would be quite easy to lay low for a few years until we can contact our own people. Have you forgotten? We are spies before combat soldiers."

His men perked up at another mission only this time long term. Plus, humans were quite tasty unlike Azromians.

"Hurry, we have to get off this planet before we're caught again."

They crept along the rubble in tight formation towards the platform for the gateway console, hoping it was still intact. When they arrived, jubilation swept over them to see that it was. The communications officer quickly went to work unjamming the console and setting their alternate coordinates for Earth.

From below came the sound of boots hitting the corridor and they knew it was now or never. Making sure they were ready, the group watched the vortex open in front of them. As they stepped in, ten Azrom soldiers came charging across the platform. Leading them was Talas with one arm outstretched as if trying to grab hold of them from that distance.

"No!" Talas yelled.

Sars turned to him, baring a row of sharp pointy teeth and hissed before being swallowed by the vortex. It closed shut after the last Razznian crossed over the threshold, seconds before Talas could get there.

Azrom's soil lay soaked with Razznian blood. Those who survived were being hauled into a large vehicle to be taken deep into the mines. Some of the Razznians got away from the fighting and a search was underway. The air was still full of heat from the cannons blasts and it intensified the smell of blood.

General Kur walked the battlefield checking bodies to see if there were any Azrom soldiers still breathing. His own body was covered in Razznian blood and he hated the feel of it. This was not aesthetically pleasing by any means. He did say let there be blood, just not on him.

A figure off in the distance steadily advanced towards him and when he could make out who it was, he saw Rass, also covered in blood with a smile across his face. The fight was his ideal arena; vicious and messy. His right arm was still morphed into a giant claw, the tips dragging on the ground.

"Did you have fun, General?" Kur called out.

"Oh, I did." Rass retracted his claw, becoming an arm once again and wiped his mouth with a bloody hand. Kur cringed. "I take it this wasn't to your liking?"

"Obviously. How fairs our supreme ruler?"

"Incensed," Rass replied stopping a few feet from Kur. "His palace has been scarred."

"Along with his pride. That plan he executed just now was brilliant."

"I wonder about that," Rass tapped his lip with a finger. Kur wanted to smack his hand dripping with blood away.

"Regardless, we still have some of those creatures on the loose."

"We'll find them."

Razzna

The moment a vortex appeared in Razzna's system, Lord Kraznan was alerted. At first, he was in a state of disbelief, then he realized what it meant. He didn't need to see the beam traveling through it to know where the situation was headed. This miscalculation on his part would now be the ruin of his race if he didn't figure something out quickly.

"Launch all of the remaining ships and make sure they hold as many of our people as possible."

There was a long pause that followed as he watched his councilmen stare in shock.

"WE are not abandoning Razzna!"

A sigh of relief filled the room. He knew what they were thinking and rightly so.

"That blast will devastate our world, make no mistake about it. But, we will leave for now and wait for the aftermath to settle down."

"Will we take vengeance on our enemy?"

"Vengeance? I believe we attacked them based on that Lassian whore's suggestion."

"It did seem sound at the time, my Lord."

"Umm, yes it did. We have lost too much in this battle. Time to reassess our agenda. How long before it hits?"

"At its current speed, ten days. This way, your majesty. Your flagship awaits."

Lord Kraznan stood up from his throne and slid proudly down the middle of the room to the entryway. He would save the rest of his race, making the vow even as he reached the hangar.

On board the flagship, every soldier scrambled to complete their checklists and get the engines running. A bright light could be seen in the middle of the vortex and contact was imminent. Lord Kraznan watched thousands of ships leave the planet surface and take to the darkness of space. They barely had enough time to get out of range so traveled at top speed to create a small cushion of safety. The flagship lifted off to join them.

The population of Razzna stood silent on each ship when they stopped near the second planet from their own. With deep sadness and horror, they witnessed the beam shoot out of the vortex and head straight for Razzna. A bright ball of fire spread across an entire region, altering the face of the planet. The vortex collapsed inward and snapped shut.

A soldier had come running into the cannon operations chamber nearly sputtering. Halfar had to backhand the man to calm him down. When he relayed his report of Talas going to the gateway in pursuit of Razznians, he couldn't believe it. Now he stood on the platform with the rest of all parties involved staring at the Lassian warrior.

"How did you know?" Halfar asked Talas in a state of confusion.

"It dawned on me that the imprisoned Razznians could have broken out with the others except he kept his team with him in the holding cell. Which means, he was planning to be rescued and return home. Since you fired on Razzna, communication would be impossible and the gateway had been locked down. The only other way out would be to send themselves to Earth. They already had an alternate route, remember?"

Modas frowned at him then. Halfar wondered what made the manbeast hate the Lassian warrior so much even when it benefitted their race. Rass came up from behind the royal guards and stood in front of Talas.

"I too realized it around the same time as you, but I was not close enough."

"Apparently neither was I," Talas sighed heavily. "I missed them by seconds."

"At least we know where they went. Can we get the coordinates from the console?" Halfar asked the guardian.

"I can, and I will." The guardian went down on one knee and bowed his head low. "I am deeply ashamed to have left my post to defend my fellow soldiers."

"Get up!" Halfar snapped. "We were in the midst of battle! There is no way you could have known this would happen!"

"Since the gateway is unlocked, we can open a pathway to New Lassa and see how they're faring." Talas suggested. "It seems you have Azrom under control."

"This battle was far too short and uninspiring. I expected more from them." Halfar stated as he nodded to the guardian to complete the task. "Well, maybe the battle on New Lassa will be more exciting for you," Kur said his tone dripping with sarcasm. Halfar knew he was angry by the number of casualties and felt the same. This was not the time.

"Open it," Halfar commanded.

He wanted to make sure Chardon and his son were safe. If the planet was overrun with Razznians he would make sure to kill every last one. The gate opened, and the group walked through.

As they set foot on New Lassa, they all gasped at the devastation causing them to choke on the sizzling air. Modas stood still, a multitude of emotions conveying on his face. Talas slumped down to the ground on the back of his legs. Halfar's pupils burned red and his hands balled into fists. Kur and Rass scanned the vicinity for signs of life. The planet surface was in ruins.

Talas got a taste of the dust in the crackling air and his eyes went wide. He clambered up on his feet and stumbled towards a dark patch on the ground. Using his finger, he ran it across and it came up slightly sticky. The smell confirmed that it was Razznian remains. Another dark patch a few feet away made him weep for it was Lassian blood he smelled.

"Gone," he whispered.

Modas grabbed him by the front of his jacket.

"What do you mean, gone?" His anger was palpable.

"Disintegrated." Talas held up his fingers smudged with both remains.

Modas got a whiff and pushed him away.

There was no sound. It was as if the planet had ceased all activity.

"What did this?" Halfar demanded.

He too had crouched down at a dark patch and tested its contents.

Modas gritted his teeth and clinched his fists.

"Chardon."

They all looked at him incredulous, except Talas. Halfar went paler than usual and Kur feared he might falter.

"How?" He asked.

Talas stood up.

"Chardon is our leader because he has more power than any of us put together. You could say he is a walking planet bomb."

He covered his face with his hands and quietly sobbed. The Azromians turned their heads to let him grieve in peace.

Modas looked off into the distance and saw a mound directly in the center of the aftermath. His vision zeroed in on it and without warning, sped towards it. Talas removed his hands sensing the manbeast's motion and tracked the direction he was heading. At once, the entire group followed.

Sliding to a halt, Modas held himself like a statue as he peered down at the hunched over body. With shaky hands he reached out to feel for any sign of life. There was a faint pulse felt against his fingers from touching the back of the neck. He bent down and went to raise the head.

"Stop!" Talas made it to his side and clamped a hand on Modas wrist. The manbeast smacked his hand away and growled. "You can't move him! Look!"

Against his better judgment, Modas finally saw Chardon's limbs fused together along with his head to his knees. Halfar crawled to Chardon, his hand shaking a mere inch from his hair, not daring to touch him. Talas ran his fingers through his own hair and grabbed hold, tight.

Dark dust swirling around like a storm came barreling towards them, a medical cruiser in its center. At its helm was Ganna with four medics onboard, all wearing protective cloaks and face covering. She came to a screeching halt and they climbed out of the vehicle.

"Step away!" She yelled breathlessly.

"You're alive," Talas spoke, releasing his tresses.

"Of course, I am," Ganna snapped. "We all evacuated into the underground bunkers."

"What underground bunkers?" Talas yelled back.

"The ones I decided to have installed when this battle was brought up. Chardon approved it and made it clear to only use them if necessary."

Ganna knelt in front of Chardon and pursed her lips. She motioned for her assistants. "We have to lift him up like this without jarring the body. Come." She placed a hand on Halfar's shoulder. "You need to step away."

Halfar only nodded and inched backwards a few feet. They watched the medics gently carry Chardon and place him in a pod secured in the hatch at the back of the cruiser. Ganna reclaimed her seat at the control and sped off.

"Can you follow her?" Kur asked Modas. Modas snapped out of his despair and turned angry eyes at the Azrom General. "Lead the way."

Ahead of them, the ground opened like a lid being removed from a box. A ramp led down and Ganna's cruiser disappeared inside. Fearing the entrance would close, the group ran towards it, making it in time before it did. The ramp was long, taking them on a nearly one-hour trek to reach the bottom. Double doors slid open and revealed hundreds of Lassians inside.

"How many bunkers are there?" Talas asked no one. His amazement clear.

"Over a hundred," a familiar voice answered.

Talas looked over to see Kelin, battered and bruised but alive, walking to him. A sheepish grin was fixated on his face.

"You're here."

"You didn't think I died, did you? I'm stronger than that," Kelin wrapped his arms around him and squeezed tight. "I'm glad to see you too," he whispered in Talas' ear.

"I…" Talas begin.

"Shh. There's no need."

Kelin released him and straightened his posture.

"This bunker has most of the council and those who were closest to the gateway. The ones with enhanced speed tried to save as many as possible before Chardon went all nuclear."

Halfar pushed his way forward and demanded, "Where has Ganna taken Chardon?"

"The medical lab. She had one built in each bunker but this one is fully equipped."

Halfar turned and charged into the direction he thought the lab might be and ran into Jakar who blocked his path. The manbeast stared blankly down at him.

"Move away, manbeast!"

Jakar's eyes darkened, making Halfar step back.

"You will not interfere with Chardon's recovery. There is nothing you can do."

"Father!" Farin's high pitched voice rang across the bunker. Halfar turned around and was hit in the mid-section by Farin ramming into him. He knelt to his son's level and stroked his head. "Mother is hurt. I can feel it," Farin cried, his voice muffled by Halfar's body.

Lifting Farin's head up, he found a haggard child with dark circles under his eyes and a paler complexion than normal. One of the female workers came over and took the boy's hand, guiding him away.

"Come, young one. You need to rest." She gave Halfar a nod as she walked away.

"Where is your mother?" Modas asked Jakar. The edge in his tone made his son blink.

"At the far end."

"Is she hurt?"

"Yes," Jakar said.

Modas made his way down the aisle, going further into the bunker.

Making sure no one else was in ear shot, Kelin motioned for the rest of the group to join him to the side. A few Lassians glanced over but did not continue their scrutiny.

"Why are you here?" He hissed at them. "What happened? It must have been really bad."

Kelin met each one's gaze. They took turns relaying the situation and Kelin's eyes grew wider with each report. When they were finished, he leaned against a wall and slump down. Talas tried to comfort him.

"It seems we are not needed on New Lassa after all," Kur proclaimed. "Our wounded can stay here until the recover. We have work to do on Azrom."

"I'm not leaving," Halfar snapped.

"No one suggested you should," Rass added, "My Lord."

"Is there anyone who can open the gateway?" Kur inquired of the occupants in the bunker.

A lone male stood up and headed towards them. "I am one of the guardians." He lowered his head. "I am the last guardian. The other three are gone."

"That is unfortunate," Rass shook his head. "Let's get going."

"It would be faster with a cruiser," the Lassian suggested.

"Can one hold all of us?"

Rass gestured to the royal guards who accompanied them.

"Of course."

Once the entourage was on the opposite side of the bunker's entrance, Talas sat down next to Kelin and rested his head on his shoulder. They sat quietly for a long time,

Jakar watching them, curious. Realizing there was an audience, Talas sat up and faced Kelin.

"This is bad, my love."

Kelin nodded in agreement. He glanced sideways at him and managed a smile.

"It could have been a whole lot worse." Kelin sighed. "But, we won."

"Did we?" Talas pondered.

Jakar moved, startling the two lovers. His large frame loomed over them like a giant wall of flesh. "You need to see my mother."

"Yes, I guess I better," Talas replied. "As tacticians, we have to assess the outcome."

"This way."

Talas and Kelin followed the manbeast down the same path as Modas to see Jaron.

Lying flat on her back staring at the ceiling, Jaron remained silent as Modas stood scrutinizing every inch of her body. The facial expression said it all. He was not happy. Although the wounds were minimal, Jaron was spent of energy. She had use everything within her to rescue her people, going at speeds she didn't even know she could achieve. Hearing footsteps coming down the aisle she slowly turned her head to see. Even that felt like a chore.

She watched her son, Jakar, extend an arm directing Talas to her.

He looks like warmed over wild beast kill.

Jaron wanted to laugh at him but was too weak. Instead, she narrowed her eyes in disgust at him. From the side of her vision she saw Modas do the same.

"Really, love? Not glad to see me alive?"

Talas tried to joke. It came out deadpan.

Jaron licked her dry cracked lips and a raspy, almost guttural voice came out in a whisper. "Of course, I'm glad you're alive, you twit. I was attempting to act natural."

Talas reached over and clasped her hand, squeezing it softly.

"I'm glad to see you too."

Jaron looked over at Modas.

"Can you leave us for a bit?" Modas did not like that request and remained. "Modas," she hissed through gritted teeth. "We don't have time for your rivalry nonsense."

That stirred him, and he quickly left, angry. Talas nodded to Kelin and his lover walked back to the other side of the bunker.

"Now, tell me what the hell happened."

Recuperation

Weeks after the battle both Azrom and New Lassa were still trying to mend their people and their planet. Halfar traveled back to Azrom only once to oversee the palace repairs. He stayed next to Chardon's sleeping form in the medical recovery bay on New Lassa. Ganna was able to get Chardon to shift into female form, it being the stronger gender, and forced the limbs to detach from each other. It had taken nearly ten days for her body to completely lay flat.

A movement out of the corner of his eye jarred Halfar out of his half slumber. The doors had opened and Farin came in by himself. At first, Halfar was concerned that his son was wondering around without supervision then he remembered. His son had claws to defend himself if necessary. The other thing was that no one on New Lassa would harm him, save Ganna.

"Father!" Farin rushed over to him and climbed in this lap. "Mother hasn't woken up yet?" He placed his small hands on the chamber lid.

"Not yet, little one."

"It should be any day now," Ganna hollered out from across the room, startling them both.

Halfar had forgotten she was in there with him.

Farin smiled at that. Halfar felt tired. More tired than he had ever felt in his entire life. Is this what love does to you? The emotions alone were almost too much for him to bear. He questioned whether it was worth all this.

"Come," he lifted Farin off his lap and down onto the floor. "Let's go outside."

The air no longer had a static sizzling effect, making it okay to wander the surface for longer periods of time. Most of the fields were gone along with the wild life but most were saved by the scientific council members before the battle began. A haze lurked all around, minimizing the warmth and appearance of the sun. Workers were out tilling the ground to prepare for replanting, the dark splotches of remains no longer visible.

As father and son walked leisurely, Halfar caught a glimpse of some- thing in the sky above and his gaze fell on the giant monolith somehow untouched, standing majestic as high as the mountains. Planted on top was a manbeast with hands on hips staring out at the horizon, his back towards them so Halfar couldn't see his face. There was no need, it being Trinon, carefree as ever.

Farin pouted. "I wanna' climb it too."

Halfar raised an eyebrow and looked down on Farin's shiny black nails then the monolith.

"Maybe there's a trick to getting your claws to dig into it."

He watched his son's face light up with hope, which he had none for that happening.

For the first time, Halfar explored some of New Lassa and found it lacking by far from the Lassians original home world. Fresh pain crept up inside him knowing he was to blame. Sending a planet bomb out of spite from being rejected was childish and there was no way for him to fix it. Half the population had been wiped out in an instant.

He thought of his own planet, Azrom, with its many troubles and the tiredness came over him again. Farin tugged at his tunic sleeve and he realized he had stopped walking. Smiling, he continued until they reached a cruiser hub. They were going to do a bit more exploring. He felt duty bound to do so.

Multicolored lights flickered on the control panel of the recovery chamber and when they stopped, the hatch release with a loud hiss, sliding down to reveal its occupant. For a moment, Chardon laid still, taking in her surroundings and deduced that she was in Ganna's medical facility. It appeared a bit different though. Anxiety gripped her. Was New Lassa destroyed? Is this a new temporary place? Her hands balled up into fists.

"Are you going to lie there all day?"

Ganna's voice traveled to her.

Slowly, Chardon lifted herself into a sitting position. Bile rose up in her throat and she projectile vomited across the edge of the healing capsule onto the floor. She slumped forward shaking from the assault and in awe of its strength, sapping hers in return.

"Oh, my!"

Ganna pressed an icon on the wall and within seconds, two medical assistants came rushing in.

"Please tend to that mess over there. It seems our leader is still not feeling well."

While the assistants went to work, Ganna came over with a cloth for Chardon and wiped the residual from her mouth. Not a drop had gotten on the rest of her body. Chardon stared at her, leery as to her motives because she was sure the scientist had no remorse whatsoever for all that transpired.

"Let's get you some robes, shall we?" Ganna smiled and went to the cabinet where she kept fresh ones.

"How long?" Chardon asked in a raspy voice.

Talking made her throat hurt more.

"Hmm, about ten weeks."

Ganna came back with a robe.

"I must say, you recuperated much faster than I could have imagined."

"Is that so?" Chardon tried clearing her throat.

"Oh, and Halfar has been by your side most of the time."

Chardon's head snapped up.

"Where is he?"

"Out mapping our decrepit planet to see what can be done for it."

"Where are we?" Chardon asked in a panic.

Ganna gave her a funny look.

"Is there something wrong with your long-term recall?"

"We're on New Lassa?" Chardon was shocked.

"Of course, we are! Why would," Ganna trailed off and pursed her lips. "As powerful as you are, Chardon, you cannot destroy an entire planet." Ganna huffed. "Tone your arrogance."

Small tingles erupted in Chardon's fingers and she knew why. Her body instinctively wanted to murder that woman. The sensation ceased just as quickly, her body too weak to conjure up enough deadly energy for the task.

The doors slid open and Halfar came swiftly in, nearly bulldozing Ganna to the ground. He wrapped his arms around Chardon's naked body and breathed in her scent. She couldn't return his affection and it frustrated her. Seeing the robe, he shook it out and managed to get it on her.

"How are you feeling?" He asked, concern on his face.

"Like I died." She saw him go pale and laughed at him. It was short lived, her body rejecting the act. "I'm so weak," Chardon whispered softly and felt tears sting her eyes.

Halfar gently lifted her out of the capsule and held her to him. Ganna was about to protest when Halfar turned and stared at her. Chardon could only imagine what kind of look the Azromian ruler had given the woman. Ganna backed away and let them pass.

In the hallway outside the medical bay, Chardon got a first glimpse of the bunker. She had known about Ganna's idea to build them but never knew the specifics. As Halfar carried her through the different areas she was struck by the sheer size of it.

"Are we going outside?" Halfar halted and Chardon was once again uneasy.

"Not today," Halfar replied. "You need to take it slow."

"I've been down for ten weeks," Chardon tried to sound angry. Her lack of strength prevented it.

"Which is a miracle in itself that you are awake."

"Tell me," Chardon pleaded.

She wanted to know the damage and she could see he knew what she was asking.

"Not today," he said again and walked on until he came to a doorway.

The doors slid open and Chardon grimaced at the sterile white of the room. Breaking up the monotony were red and brown coverings on the bed along with golden plush pillows, no doubt Halfar's aesthetics. He set her down on it, his body going with hers. They lay there, Chardon wrapped in his arms, for a long time.

"You will tell me," Chardon demanded weakly.

"Or what?" Halfar laughed softly.

"I won't let you touch me ever again."

Halfar turned to look at her and his eyes narrowed.

Be angry all you want, Chardon yelled silently before drifting off into another deep sleep.

Moving Forward

Fields of golden stalks and vegetation covered much of New Lassa as the surface went through reparations. Growing food was the main priority with housing second. The air quality had equalized in important sectors, the rest remained in a static like haze. Policies for population increase were implemented soon after the first harvest when the census showed another devastating toll on the Lassian race.

Each bunker was emptied out in small batches as parts of the planet became livable again. Chardon sat on a hilltop, propped up by her elbows with both legs bent up. Since coming out of her death sleep she was unable to shift back to her male form. According to Ganna, it stemmed from the amount of energy she exerted. Only time would be the remedy. She scanned the horizon and feeling a breeze, let her head flop back as she closed her eyes.

"I don't have to tell you that your mate has gone insane, do I?"

The voice had a condescending lilt to it and Chardon recognized it as Jaron's. She opened her eyes to find Jaron's face leaning over her as she stared. Dark patches were still visible underneath her cousin's eyes and the smile was strained.

"He is just being overprotective," Chardon replied.

"To think you and Farin are safer on Azrom is a special kind of stupidity."

Jaron sat down next to her, assuming a similar position on the hilltop. She too reveled in the soft breeze as Chardon had.

"He is no more than your mate," Chardon chided. "Modas wants to lock you away and destroy the key."

"Modas needs to get over the fact that I too am a Lassian warrior. I fight when it is necessary just like he does."

"So, my brilliant cousin, what plans did you and Talas come up with?"

"We think a negotiation with Razzna is in order." Chardon turned and stared at her. Jaron continued. "Of course, Halfar does not agree. But, the truth is he has no say since he has ruined yet another planet."

"Why are we negotiating with the enemy?"

"Sestis set in motion an ill crafted, although quite elaborate, scheme that I don't think neither side took the time to question. The Razznians are a reptilian race and does not have the means to mine their resources. Rumor has it their automated system malfunctioned, so they had to resort to manual labor. Their bodies are not made for it and that is why they have been enslaving other beings to work them."

"Are you suggesting we give them some of our man-beasts? After all this?"

Chardon sat straight, a flash of anger across her face.

"No!" Jaron snapped. "I am not saying that! What is wrong with you?" Chardon flinched from the voracity in her voice. "We can get them an audience with some of the worker trade networks."

"Razzna is in no shape for anything right now. We don't even know if their mines are still intact."

"Considering how deep they are, it is safe to assume they are. If we start soon, they will be prepared when the planet surface is cleared enough for them to return."

Chardon felt a twinge of jealousy. She was the leader of her race, yet had not come to such a simple deduction. There were times when her plans turned out being the best. Ninety percent of the time, it was Jaron or Talas who exceled at strategy and logistics.

"She didn't win," Chardon stated, referencing Sestis.

"You must be joking," Jaron scoffed. "SHE won a few rounds." She glanced over at Chardon. "Are you going to inform your mate of your condition?"

Chardon also glanced down at her midsection and sighed. Halfar being stubborn and prone to bouts of childish tantrums, caved in after a few months of her denying his advances. He told her everything and within days had impregnated her.

"That monster is starting to have an affinity for breeding. I'll tell him when he comes for another visit," Chardon answered.

"We are on a breeding initiative. You are no exception."

"But you are?" Chardon eyed her with mild contempt.

"I have thirteen offspring, Chardon, how many do you have?"

"Noted." Chardon got up and brushed flecks of yellow grass off her robes. "Anyone else contributing to the cause?"

Jaron smiled up at her.

"Oh yes, Mara found a field worker to play with and is with child. And," Jaron paused, her smile widening. Chardon tilted her head to one side. "It seems Kelin has finally done his due diligence."

"Talas?" Chardon asked incredulous. Jaron nodded in acknowledgement. "The drama!"

"Exactly. I am going to steer clear for a while." Jaron also stood. "There is something else you should know." Her face became serious. "The Dreridians want compensation for the podsuits Sestis commissioned for the Razznians. If something cannot be agreed upon," Jaron stopped.

"You're joking?"

Now Chardon was angry. Angrier than she had felt in a long time. "We can't sustain another battle with any race, let alone one three times more advanced than we are."

"Lucky for us, we have Azrom as an ally who also has a grudge against them for plotting with Sestis to infiltrate the planet."

"Halfar didn't take that too lightly. And neither do I, for Razznian ships invading our new planet, forcing me to damage it far more than I wanted to."

"We have a lot to do, leader." Jaron walked back down the hill from whence she came leaving Chardon to contemplate the course their race had taken.

Villages surrounding the royal palace lay in various states of destruction giving the once majestic structure, now in shambles, the appeal of an ancient ruin. Survivors stumbled through the wreckage searching for remnants of their lives. They never had much but what they did have, they cherished. Some were left with no home to return to.

In the palace, the royals breathed a sigh of relief for being spared any real damage. Only the main structure of the palace had been hit, sparing the attached buildings that housed the royal family and their staff. Construction from inside was ongoing and nearly complete with concentration on the outside being last on the list.

General Kur was not onboard with this decision. He felt it was all about aesthetics and having their people see a decrepit palace did not fare well for morale. Even from a distance he could tell some of the villagers were looking up, wondering what would become of their race. It still made him shiver with rage whenever he thought of the audacious plan the Razznians carried out.

Standing in the newly built battle chamber adjacent to the completely redone command center, he waited for Halfar and Rass to join him. After speaking with Talas and Jaron regarding the Dreridians via the communication screen, he had relayed the information to Halfar. A deadly silence had ensued afterwards and then he was ordered to wait here. Four altered enforcers stood at each corner of the room, courtesy of the science division that kept all the data on the last batch he had created for the battle on Earth decades ago.

A loud hiss made him look up. Halfar came charging in, face scrunched up, with Rass in tow looking bored. His supreme ruler stopped short of the console sitting in the middle of the chamber and eyed the enforcers.

"Why are those here? Better yet, where did they come from?"

Kur folded his arms across his chest and cocked his head to one side playfully.

"Why, my Lord, have you forgotten about my pets?" Halfar was not amused. "I had them ordered two cycles ago. These four are part of the first batch."

"I destroyed them for a reason!" Halfar snapped. "They are an abomination!"

"Yet very much needed if we have to go up against Dreridians."

Rass flipped his cloak back over his shoulders so that it lay behind him and laid one hand on the hilt of his longsword. Kur knew what he was waiting for and continued.

"If you think for one moment I would let you or your pet general destroy my soldiers, you are mistaken." He saw Halfar's expression turn to disbelief and Rass stared at him in anger at the 'pet general' reference. "You seemed to have lost focus and made emotion-based decisions detrimental to our race. I will not allow it, supreme ruler or not."

Kur bent his upper body backwards, feeling the air of Halfar's dark claws snap shut mere inches from his face. Rass immediately sprung to action and wedged himself between the two. He turned to glare at Kur, the message was clear. This is not the time. Kur exhaled through his nose and resigned his offensive stance. Both were on the same page and he wondered why Rass was delaying the inevitable.

"Let's not, shall we?" Rass cooed. "We are here for the greater good of Azrom, correct?" Halfar, still seething, retracted his claws. "I believe we have a more pressing matter to discuss."

"I will not give those monsters salvation or any kind of helping hand. Razzna deserved what I gave it!" Halfar shouted in defiance.

"There is a bigger picture here." Kur sighed. "We also have to deal with Razznians on Earth."

"No need to worry about that. I received information that another alien race has set up shop within the crime industry's reconnaissance and are willing to take in my officers from before."

Kur's eyes went wide. "You have your officers from Earth? Are they not too old for such a task now?"

Halfar snorted and pivoted to stride towards the other side of the console. "I had them put in stasis. They will be just as fresh as they were back then. Like no time had passed."

Kur placed a hand across his eyes and squeezed them shut as he rubbed his temples. It was the Lassian catastrophe all over again, this time with Earthlings.

Halfar had a hard time letting go of the things he wants.

"And the Dreridians?" He asked his Lord.

"Oh, I have something in mind for them." Halfar's voice dripped with venom.

"And that is?"

"I do not have to relay every one of my agendas to you!"

"As the general of the royal guards and the Armada, I need to know anything pertaining to battles that utilize our forces, so yes you do."

"My Lord," Rass cleared his throat as he bowed slightly. Halfar turned on him and they nearly shared the same breath. "Your new council is waiting. It was your destination before this news came about."

Halfar backed away from him and looked over at Kur.

"We must leave. This discussion will be resumed after," Halfar said. "Along with the issue of your insubordination."

Kur followed the two out of the chamber and in the hall exchanged a glance with Rass.

Patience.

The eight houses of Azrom's royal family assembled in the great hall where they, along with all the councilmen, awaited their supreme ruler's arrival. A tense atmosphere permeated the room, remnants of the Razznian assault that left Azrom in disarray. Anger blended with disappointment filled everyone's minds.

At long last, footsteps echoed outside the entrance and Halfar appeared with his entourage in tow. His fierce expression spoke volumes. He too was quite angry and frustrated. They rounded the corner and stormed down the aisle to his throne. Kur and Rass flanked him as he dropped down on it.

Two councilmen approached the bottom of the throne's platform and bowed. They glanced at each other and when they rose, the one on the left began speaking.

"My Lord, we have gone over the reports and would like to express our concerns regarding the Dreridian issue."

"Is that so? What are your concerns?"

He eyed the room and saw many of the councilmen and royals fidgeting.

"We agree that they must be held accountable for their part in assisting the Razznians. But, given their technological expertise, it would throw us into a new war we are not willing to endure."

"Are you suggesting we not avenge our planet and let them slide?" Halfar sneered.

"No one is saying that!" One of the royal princes snapped.

Halfar looked over to see who it was. His cousin, Lord Romnus, stood apart from the rest of the family. Where Halfar was tall and slender, Romnus was taller and well built. His biceps bulged against his tunic even with his arms relaxed. Dark hair not entirely straight cascaded past his shoulders.

"Then what would you have us do, cousin?" Halfar spat.

"Think about the strain this would cause on our race."

The other councilman in front of the throne cleared his throat.

"What we propose is opening negotiations with the Dreridians."

"That is not an option," Halfar replied shutting down the notion.

A heavy silence swept the hall and some of the councilmen were visibly shaken with rage. Halfar didn't care what they thought. He was the supreme ruler and his word was definitive.

"I will not leave my offspring a legacy of cowardice and defeat!"

"Why bring Farin into this?"

"It isn't just Farin," Halfar yelled. "I have another who will be born soon enough. Azrom must show might!"

This time, there was no cheer of congratulations. Instead, a kind of resentment. The royal family rose in defiance and exited the hall, much to Halfar's surprise. He couldn't believe they had done such a thing. Before he could protest, the two councilmen raised their hands up in surrender.

"My Lord, please do not be offended. These have been troubling times for all of us. Forgive them." They bowed low.

The elder councilman moved forward and also bowed low in front of Halfar.

"I think the topic is too heated for the moment. We should revisit it at a later time, if that is to your liking."

Halfar sat back in his throne and gripped the armrests. Kur leaned over and whispered, "Let it be, for now." He relaxed his body and pushed himself off the throne. Standing above his audience he glared at them.

While the remaining councilmen bowed low, Halfar strode down the aisle with his two generals and four royal guards. No one uttered a word as he passed by them. As his entourage left the hall, turning the corner then down the corridor, so did most of the council.

Three councilmen and five advisors stayed behind in the hall and gathered near the throne. The first to speak was a councilman and he did not mince words.

"That tyrant will get us all killed!"

"Our race is in jeopardy," the second one added.

"And what's this about a new spawn from that Lassian he mated with?"

"The royal bloodline is getting tainted."

One of the advisors rubbed his jaw, contemplating, then said, "We can remedy that easy enough."

With looks of horror, the others stared at him.

"You're not suggesting we murder his offspring?" The fourth advisor exclaimed.

"Keep your voice down," the second hissed.

"Of course not!" The third snapped. "I am merely saying, if we can convince our ruler to create a child of pure Azrom blood that would be ideal."

"And the two half breeds?" The fourth asked.

"They can be married off into one of the lower royal families." He waved his hand dismissively.

"Well, with that decided, we can now focus on a new war." The third councilman sighed.

"It's not like we can't win. We are Azromian warriors." The first retorted.

The eight walked out of the hall through the side entrance that lead out to the other side of the palace. There was much more planning to do, the direst being reeling their ruler in to bend at their will.

END

Excerpt from

Bonds
of
Contrition

Core Book 3

FRESH STARTS

New Lassa

"Ten years," Chardon, the leader of New Lassa, sighed.

In female form, Chardon stood leaning over the window sill of her new chamber staring out at the fairly revived landscape. The Razznian battle ships that had invaded her planet left many sectors in ruins. To ensure the planet's survival, Chardon added insult to injury by using her powers to wipe out everything. The blast traveled like a wave across the planet, disintegrating plants, flesh and machine. Most of her race were saved from it by taking refuge in underground bunkers designed to withstand it.

She forced her dark blue eyes to adjust in order to see farther across the land. Off in the distance Jaron was scolding Trinon who had to look down at his mother. He stood with that disarming smile on his face which infuriated everyone, even her.

A loud galloping sound came from the corridor outside her chamber and she hung her head in anticipation. Only one ball of energetic species made that kind of ruckus. The door flew open, banging against the wall.

Standing out of breath, black hair whipped around like snakes, was her own child Farin. He wore his usual black body tunic with cloak and shiny leather boots. His pale creamy skin and murky green eyes, which he inherited from his father, were in stark contrast. Nearly the same height as his mother, he was tall and beautiful at the age of twenty.

"Mother!"

"Yes, Farin?"

"I did it!"

Chardon turned to lean back against the window.

"Did what, Farin?"

He grinned. "I climbed the monolith!" Taking a deep breath and exhaling, he said, "And I did it just as fast as Trinon!"

So that's what happened.

Chardon now understood why Jaron was chastising Trinon. Farin was not a manbeast but he did have shiny black talons able to cut through nearly anything. Because of their sleekness, he could never get a grip on the giant slate that stood as high as a mountain. All the manbeasts practiced on it. She could only imagine the damage done to its surface by Farin's exuberance.

"Is that so?" Chardon crossed her arms and waited.

She didn't have to wait long. Her bodyguard, and Trinon's father, Modas, came into the room looking none too happy. A quick glance at her followed by a short bow was all she got before he launched into his complaint.

"Your child sliced through most of the monolith trying to climb it," Modas said through gritted teeth.

"So I heard."

"We need someone who can repair it before it starts to shift from the cracks and collapses."

"Aren't you being overdramatic?"

"No," Modas replied. His teeth still clenched. "I am not."

Farin's excited expression turned to dread and Chardon almost felt bad for her silly son. What made her not pay it any mind was Modas' behavior on the matter. He had been going off the rails lately and everyone made attempts to keep him in check. All nearly seven feet of his frame shook with indignation.

"I will see to it." Chardon pushed herself from the window sill and walked over to him. "It is a piece of slab, Modas, regardless of how many generations it has served your species."

That snapped him out of his current state and into one that Chardon found even more offensive: Disgust. It was a 'how dare you' look. A high-pitched whimper from the doorway made the manbeast jerk his head towards Farin. Chardon saw the realization in Modas' eyes and was not surprised when he turned away and strode right out the door.

"Don't worry, Farin. You did nothing wrong. Come."

Chardon opened her arms and Farin ran into them. They stood in an embrace for a moment. When they released each other, both laughed. Further down the corridor, Modas heard their laughter and fumed.

He didn't find it amusing by any means. The monolith was

one of the few things salvaged from their original home world and transferred to New Lassa. It had been a training tool for manbeasts for probably centuries, maybe even millennia. No one knew where it came from or how it came to be. Even their hated head scientist, Ganna, had no answers.

Up ahead he watched Trinon walk off away from his mother, unfazed by the lecture. His older brother, Mota, met him and slapped the young manbeast on the back in jest. They had no sense of pride for their history. Both only looked forward and cared nothing for the past. Modas eyes narrowed. They would have to face the past soon enough. His agenda was coming to fruition.

An infant appeared mere centimeters from his face and he stared into the pouty lips of his newly born grandchild who his daughter, Mara, held up proudly. The litter she had been born in had three beast and two energy users. She was, of course, not a manbeast so could never under- stand the plight of man- beasts but he loved her just the same. Grabbing the Lassian child from his daughter's hands, Modas lifted him up higher for closer inspection.

General Kur surveyed the palace grounds from his balcony on the fourth level. He swept his forest green hair off his shoulders and smiled at the progress that had been made. Ten years since the Razznians, attacked Azrom and the planet surface was still in near ruins. Rebuilding the in- side of the palace was complete with the outer wall being the last thing project for repairs. Off in the distance, he could see the villages beyond the barrier wall that separated them from the palace. It angered him to see the suffer- ing of his people knowing it all stemmed from Supreme Ruler Halfar's reign.

The first to be compensated should have been their people. At the council's behest, Halfar made reparations of the palace in its entirety a priority over everything else. Kur found his judge- ment lacking in reason. The same happened when he himself was duped by the royal council into launching a coup against Halfar while on Earth. Instead of finding the root cause, Halfar had commanded Rass to dispatch him, without consideration for their history together. Despite the cruelty of it and how Rass' decision would sway, Halfar had insisted. In the end, it only brought them closer physically and philosophically. Both were on the same page when their supreme ruler was involved.

Footsteps echoed behind him and he turned to see Rass strolling towards him, head down in deep thought. A tightening in his groin had him trying to restrain his urges. Rass aroused him often these days by simply being near, especially now with his jet black wavy hair, now down to his waist, brushing against his hips as he walked. Those small pink lips pursed in frustration made Kur lick his own. Rass finally looked up and Kur straightened his posture.

"What troubles you, general?" Kur asked playfully.

"Halfar."

"Hmm. Is he opposing some random council agenda?"

"On the contrary, he's adopting one. It is to further restrict the royal families from the main sector of the palace."

"For what reason?" Kur was suspicious.

"No clue. I have a feeling something is coming and it won't be beneficial to our race."

"That is a given." Kur tilted his head. "Bond with me."

Rass's eyes went wide and he stared at him for a long time.

"Why did you ask that?"

"Because I want you."

"Have you gone insane?" Rass seethed.

Kur stepped closer to him. They locked eyes.

"No." He ran his fingers in Rass's hair. "I want you and no one else."

"This is not the time," Rass whispered.

"When will it be?" Kur snapped. He took a breath. "There is no reason to wait."

He watched the conflict on Rass' face then saw clarity. Rass sighed heavily.

"Then I will be yours."

Filled with a sense of relief and jubilation Kur grabbed Rass by the hair and kissed him roughly. He had waited so long to ask that he had feared it would be too late to claim him. Now there were no obstacles. Figuring out what the concept of love encompassed had given him a new understanding of his feelings for Rass.

"You do realize we cannot announce it yet?" Rass said when Kur released him from his grip.

"I know."

All too well.

Halfar would not be happy. In fact, Kur figured there would be a sense of jealousy and that was the last thing he needed; Halfar declaring war on them out of spite. He used a thumb to wipe his moisture from Rass' lips then resumed viewing the palace project.

"What are you thinking?" Rass inquired, leaning over from the side.

"Our people are suffering, yet I am glad the palace is almost complete. That means we can focus on them soon."

"Don't count on that basis, Kur. I heard no intentions in the council meetings to ensure the care of our people outside the wall."

Kur turned to him and saw truth in that statement. The ones supplying the population with rations were the First Royal House and they would be the ones to deal with. This new restriction could be as a result of it. The council's and the royal's agendas did not complement each other.

"I am disappointed. We still have not resolved the issue of the Razznians on Earth either. Halfar says it is under control, but I am not so sure." Kur drummed his fingers on the ledge.

"Halfar could care less about Earth. The humans who worked for us are just keeping tabs and making sure the Razznians don't interfere in his organizations flow of revenue."

"I always hated that concept of currency. It is only one of three planets we know of that have it and those races always end up destroying themselves because of it." Kur grinned. "So, no revenge tactics?"

"He believes we have dealt a big enough blow."

"Has he forgotten the other part of the equation?" Kur asked. Rass raised an eyebrow at him. "The Dreridians. He advised us that a plan was in the works for holding them jointly responsible for the attacks."

"That plan," Rass stood up straight, "is no longer in play."

"The council," Kur snorted.

"They believe we have more important issues to attend to."

"Then, if the Razznians regroup and come back to avenge the devastation of their home world?"

"We would be wholly unprepared," Rass finished.

~END~

ABOUT THE AUTHOR

Maquel A. Jacob has had a passion for the written word since the age of seven, reading everything she could get her hands on which included encyclopedias and the thesaurus. At twelve, she had her first encounter with a Stephen King novel and was hooked. She became inspired to write her own brand of fiction. Combining multiple genres is her way of keeping things interesting.

She is also a huge Anime fan, loves a great bottle of wine and rocks out to heavy metal music. Green and lush Oregon is where she currently resides spinning imaginary worlds in her head and daydreaming.

GET READY FOR MORE GENDER SHIFTER SOCIAL SCI-FI WITH A BIT OF ROMANCE AND A TOUCH OF GORE

Find me on Facebook: MaquelAJ1
Follow me on Twitter: @MaquelAJ1
and my website:

www.maquelajacob.com